BLOOD
is the new black
A Sam Dunne Mystery

AIRSHIP 27 PRODUCTIONS

Published by Airship 27 Productions
www.airship27.com
www.airship27hangar.com

Interior illustrations © 2020 Richard Jun
Cover illustration © 2020 Rob Davis

Editor: Ron Fortier
Associate Editor: Gordon Dymowski
Marketing and Promotions Manager: Michael Vance
Production and design by Rob Davis.

ISBN: 978-1-946183-95-8

Printed in the United States of America

10 9 8 7 6 5 4 3 2 1

BLOOD is the new black

A Sam Dunne Mystery

Fred Adams Jr.

I

Darkness. Mariah's pale face stands out in the stark moonlight as she bursts from the trees into the clearing. The forest is a chiarascuro scrim behind her as her head twists from side to side, looking for somewhere to run, whipping her shoulders with her flaxen hair. Her chest heaves with frantic breath. A twig cracks, and she darts across the opening, desperate for the concealment of the shadows.

Mariah leans back against the thick trunk of an oak tree and closes her eyes, taking long breaths to slow her racing heart and quell her panic. She cocks her head one way, then the other, listening for any sound to let her know where her pursuer may be. Nothing. No sound at all, as if the forest is holding its breath.

An impossibly long arm snakes around the trunk of the tree, the hand at its end a twisted claw. Her head turns, but she sees it too late. She tries to scream, but the hand clamps over her throat, cutting off her breath and her cry. Mariah's eyes bulge from fear and duress as a body in rags follows the arm, slithering against the bark with an obscene, wet sound. The face is little more than a skull, thinly upholstered with mottled skin that glistens in the dappled moonlight. The eyes blaze red from sockets as deep as the pits of hell and lock their gaze with the terrified eyes of the captive.

The arm's mate curls like a tentacle around the other side of the trunk, a knife with a long blade like a sliver of glass in its hand. With flick of its liquid wrist, it slashes open Mariah's blouse and with a deft twist, severs her brassiere between her breasts and it falls away.

The tip of the knife traces a jagged line beneath her collarbone, blood, black in the moonlight oozing in a thick weal that drips in random rivulets over her soft white skin. He pushes his face close, dragging his lips across her chest, tasting Mariah's blood as he tastes her fear.

He pricks at her skin with the tip of the knife, as if seeking the right place to insert the blade. The mouth opens, and the last sound she hears is his coughing laughter, like the wheezing of an asthmatic. He draws back his arm for the thrust...

"Cut!"

Simon Schiff, the Producer-Director spoke, and the spell was broken.

The nasty little troll waved his arms and said, "Wrap it and move to the lake for the next shot." Everyone who had been frozen in place, silent, exploded into motion. Every person on the set grabbed something as the electrical grips unplugged power cords from the generator. Each crew member carried away a light, an umbrella diffuser, a screen, a stand or some other piece of the film gear like ants hauling cake crumbs from a picnic.

Somebody brought a robe for Lianna Smith, the blonde who played Mariah, and while part of me felt a twinge of disappointment over her covering up, the blood and violence were a real turn off. But more than enough people would shell out five bucks, or ten, or fifteen to revel in it on the big screen or the little one.

"What do you think, Sam?" Tom Willis, the screenwriter stood beside me. He was forty-two and in spite of his pipe looked like an old version of those kids I see loitering in the graphic novel section at Barnes & Noble.

"He should've said, 'Stab.'"

"We'll do the stab shot in slo-mo but never really let the audience see the blade go in. Rule one of writing horror is to show little and make the viewer fill in the blank with whatever lurks in his unconscious." He sounded like a college professor teaching Intro to Fiction. I guess he didn't know I was one too.

"I thought the whole thing was pretty creepy, especially the long arms reaching around the tree."

"I derived the image from the Monopoly Chance Card to go directly to Jail - Mr. Pennybags is dangling from the impossibly long arm of the law, actualizing the cliché. It suggests something from which there is no escape. I've seen variations on the motif in *Nightmare on Elm Street* and *Phantasm*."

I laughed. "Don't forget Gumby and Barbapapa," I said. "And Stretch Armstrong, while you're at it." Willis gave me a wounded look. "I read the script, Tom. What's the Lake Thing's motivation? Does it kill for food? For kicks? What's it do when there's nobody around to slice and dice?"

"That's the mystery," he sniffed. "Every danger loses some of its terror once its causes are understood. Konrad Lorenz wrote that, and I agree with him." He turned away and strode off before I could respond. The poor deluded bastard really thought he was creating art. When you go fishing for compliments, sometimes you reel in the hard, cold truth.

The script for *Lake Deadly* was, as Joe Bob Briggs used to say, a "basic spam in a cabin, STDH" (Stupid Teenagers Die Horribly) plot, only this time it was twenty-somethings in a tent. But the basic formula prevailed.

Schiff strutted around like Napoleon. All he needed was the hand in the placket of his coat. He'd point at something, say something quietly, and magically it would fly away. He never raised his voice at anybody; speaking softly forced everyone to pay absolute attention to him every second. When he was displeased, Schiff took people aside by the elbow and looked at them through the eyeholes of that long-suffering mask he wore for the world and spoke like a patient parent to a five-year-old. Most agreed they'd like it better if he screamed.

"Dunne," Schiff called to me and started sauntering over. I say started because he had the habit of getting somebody's attention then studiously ignoring him and making him wait for five minutes while he spoke to other people on his way over. After stopping to discuss lighting problems with Anya Savage, the DP (director of photography) and some crap about paying the caterer with Ed Leighty, his site manager, he found his way to where I was standing.

"Well, Dunne, you've seen it now." He called everyone by his or her last name, although he insisted everyone call him Simon. "What do you think?" Schiff had tousled graying brown hair and dark eyes magnified behind a pair of horn-rimmed glasses; Michael Caine *manque*.

"I think it'll sell to the splatter set."

"But can you set it to music?"

"I have a few ideas. That scene was pretty harsh. I figure the soundtrack for the tree scene should be the equivalent of striking a match, dragging it slowly across the striker until the match suddenly flares. Slow buildup to tease, and then a burst of sound about the time the hand grabs her throat."

He pondered that for a minute. His head didn't move; no sign of agreement or disapproval. "I'll have Leighty run a video of the scene over to your place tomorrow. I have a few ideas of my own. We'll see how yours and mine line up." He fired a finger pistol at me and swaggered away, calling to one of the grips, who politely stood while Simon stopped to talk to the camera man and one of the light techs.

I'd never scored a film before. My songwriting experience had been all for live performance and recording, so this game was new to me. But dealing with micromanager egos like Simon's was old business. It could go three ways: he would figure out that I can't be bought or bullied and fire me, or figure it out after I was too deeply embedded in the project to fire me conveniently, or we would settle on some sort of workable armed truce. I was hoping for number three, but I wasn't laying any bets.

I figured Simon hired me for name recognition as much as anything else; Sam Dunne, former lead guitarist of Gin Sing, solo recording artist, and the killer of Danny Barton. Old news, but people remember. When my agent Joe Mancini went over the contract for me to sign, I noticed one clause that said my name and image could be used to promote the film. I guess having a killer on staff, albeit a justified one gives street cred to an independent horror movie.

As for scoring an indie fright film, I was pretty pumped about the idea. I've been a fan of horror and sci-fi flicks for most of my forty-seven years, and the thought of actually being involved in one had a certain attraction. The up-front money, a "retainer" Leighty called it when he handed me the check, was more than I'd make teaching a bonehead English Comp class at Hanniston Area Community College (HACC to the locals), but since I had to turn down a class this semester to take the movie gig, the money was pretty much a wash.

What sweetened the deal was the residual percentage in my contract. At twelve cents a copy for DVD sales, I wouldn't get rich, but I learned long ago that residuals are the gift that keeps on giving. Not big chunks of cash, but a steady stream of small money that, combined with a lot of other small streams of money from all the other things I had going, kept me solvent. Jenny still had her job at Dora's Diner while she finished her Bachelor's degree, and the free meals would have kept me from starving to death, but I liked the thought that I paid my own way.

The entourage was moving to the lake, part of a summer camp a few miles outside my home town of Hanniston, Pennsylvania. The camp was named Camp Tuscarora after an Indian tribe, the same as one of the mountains the Turnpike tunnels through heading west. It was a coed camp with a nice setup: tennis courts, riding stable, two softball diamonds and plenty of cabins. My first thought was that *Lake Deadly* was going to be a *Friday the 13th* reprise, but Simon was ignoring the camp attributes and shooting the whole picture in the woods, being careful to keep the tennis nets and the basketball hoops out of the frame.

The cabins and other facilities did, however, make great accommodations for the film crew. Schiff's backers, Screamer Pictures, rented the place for a month, cheap in pre-season. Schiff liked to keep his crew handy day and night, but instead of taking a cabin for myself, I opted to stay in my apartment in Hanniston. Twelve miles was just enough distance to allow me to work without interference and to keep me from getting pissed off at Simon.

The lake was calm, and as if Schiff had ordered it special, a full moon reflected on the surface, making it look like one of those mirror-image jigsaw puzzles that drive you crazy because you never know which end is up, which is reality and which is the image; a metaphor for film, I guess. They were shooting a scene near the end of the script now to take advantage of the combination of the clear sky and the moon.

At the edge of the water, the camera people were taking the white balance. The tech flipped the white-screen over to show a bull's eye design for the cameraman to focus. Digital movie cameras have revolutionized film making, especially for the low-budget, independent crowd. A talented director with a high-end camera, a few lights and a good cameraman can crank out a creditable movie on a short budget with a skeleton crew. And now that I think of it, that's an apropos term for a horror film.

One of the starlets, Janine DiBasil, was standing to the side. One woman was touching up her long, dark hair, while another dabbed at her makeup. I read the script. She's the heroine, and she kills the creature from the lake, but in the last five seconds, she gets it from the creature's vengeful mate. As Frederic Brown once wrote, "for every abominable snowman, . . ."

Art Shultz, the sound tech started swearing. He turned to the camera man. "Nothing? Nothing's coming through?"

"Only a little static. No microphone."

Drawn by the sound of trouble, Schiff strode over.

"No mic," said Shultz.

"Do you have another cable?"

"Not out here."

"Then fix it." Schiff started away then turned and said, "Make it quick. We're losing the moon."

I could see by the look on Shultz's face that wasn't going to happen easily. I walked over as Shultz stood staring at the cable and grinding his teeth. "Can I help?"

"Who are you?"

"Someone with a long history of fixing cables on the fly."

He shrugged. "Be my guest."

"I'll be right back."

Shultz laughed.

"What's so funny?"

"That's what everybody says right before they get nailed in a fright film."

I jogged to my van and grabbed the tool kit I carry in my road bag. By the time I got back, everyone was pacing.

"Okay," I said, "disconnect the cable at both ends." Shultz handed me the connectors. I unscrewed the cover of the first and pulled back the insulating sleeve. I tried each of the three wires. All were solidly soldered to the terminals. The other end was the same story. Nothing disconnected.

I turned to Mike Smith, the cameraman. "You heard static?"

"Yeah, a crackling noise."

I told Shultz, "Give me the headphones and leave the camera powered up." I plugged the cable into the mic and the camera inputs. Starting at the camera end, I gave a close look to its plastic sheathing. About ten feet from the camera, I saw a sharp line where something heavy had landed on the cable. I held it between the thumb and forefinger of each of my hands, on either side of the crush mark. I gently bent the section back and forth while I listened for noise. I heard a crackling; the bad spot.

I pulled out my pocket knife and slit the sheath. Under an outer layer of braided shielding wire I found two vinyl coated lines, red and blue. I stripped the coating from the blue wire. No problem. I did the same to the red wire and found where it had frayed. The wires are multi-strand and as fine as baby hair. Step on one the wrong way or pull it too hard, and they break.

"Reach into the tool bag and grab the Burt's Bees tin at the bottom."

While he dug in the tool kit, I twisted the ends of the frayed wires.

"Is this it?"

I opened the tin and took out a piece of brass tubing, actually a half inch section of an old ball point pen refill. I pushed one piece of the broken wire into each end of the tube and crimped it shut with a pair of needle-nosed pliers.

I wrapped a small piece of electrical tape around the brass to insulate it. "Try it."

Shultz tapped the mic with his finger. It came through the headphones. "Say something."

"A, B, C—"

"You're on." I handed Shultz the phones. "It'll hold for now." He nodded, gave me a thumbs up and waved to Savage.

"Places. Scene forty-two. Light the campfire."

Shultz wrapped the mic cable a few turns around the handle and raised the boom.

Savage called, "Strike," and the high-wattage production lights came on. Someone lit the small campfire near the water's edge, and it threw flickering light on the shore.

Janine DiBasil stepped out of her robe and I could see immediately why she was the star. She had maybe the most perfect body I had ever seen, dark-nippled, gym tuned, and proportioned like a Greek statue. And yeah, she was a natural brunette. She was a beauty, and it was no wonder she had no compunction about showing it all off.

Back when I was playing lead guitar for Gin Sing, a girl might throw her bra onstage or flash the band once in a while, but I was amazed at how readily the young women in the cast took off their clothes. I was starting to believe I'd been in the wrong racket all these years. Bobby Hendricks joined her, and they looked like a contemporary version of Adam and Eve standing at the edge of the water, glowing golden in the fire light.

"Quiet on the set. Rolling. Scene twenty-seven. Take one. Action." No clack board? So much for tradition.

Janine and Bobby looked into each other's eyes for a long moment and walked hand in hand into the waist deep water, their arms went around each other. They kissed with such sweet passion that I would have believed it real if I hadn't been told by one of the grips that Bobby was gay.

In a moment, their bodies were rocking together and they were gasping. I was so busy watching the love scene that I missed the first ripples on the water behind them. A dark shape broke the surface, a misshapen head, followed by shoulders, arms and misshapen hands, one holding that wicked looking knife from the scene they'd shot earlier.

"Cut!"

Janine and Bobby stood casually as if they weren't nude and as if last two minutes had never happened. Bobby did a modest fig-leaf clutch over his privates, but Janine stood matter-of-factly, her hands at her sides. They did the scene two more times before Schiff was satisfied. "Move the camera. I want the love scene shot from behind. I want silhouettes." Schiff gave a shooing motion with his hands.

Jack Smith, the cameraman balked. "Simon, I don't think taking the camera out into the water's a good idea. We're talking ten grand here."

"So be careful. I want the shot."

"Besides, that patch in the mic wire is just taped up. It may not be waterproof."

Without missing a beat, Simon turned to a group of crew members standing to the side. "Graham." He beckoned to a chunky young woman sporting a *Walking Dead* t-shirt and hair like a rusty Brillo pad. "Hold the wire out of the water," then to the crew as a whole, "Move, people. Let's get this done."

The same scene played again, this time with Smith in waist deep water.

Graham stood dutifully holding the mic line over her head so that it never touched the surface of the lake. She was a sharp one. She held the patch in her left fist the whole time, taking no chances. I thought of the old joke: "What, and give up show business?"

Two takes later, Schiff said, "Move in close. Time for the kill scene."

Marty Barlow, the special effects guy waded out into the water. He taped the hilt of a knife and a few inches of blade, the mate of the one in the lake-thing's hand onto Bobby's back between the shoulder blades so that it stuck out perpendicular to his spine.

"Places. Rolling. Action." Bobby began gasping, his hips pumping. Janine lay back in the water, clutching his forearms. Bobby arched his back and cried out, in passion, I thought, until he bit a blood capsule and spewed stage blood from the corner of his mouth. He fell forward, pushing Janine under the water and I saw the handle of the knife sticking out of his back. Behind him the leering skull-face burst into the light.

It was very effective—in *The Seduction* when Michael Sarrazin gets stabbed in the back in the hot tub with Morgan Fairchild. Of course, this flick would be pitched to horny teeners who probably don't even remember Morgan Fairchild, let alone Michael Sarrazin, so Simon would get away with the steal.

"Cut! Places. Do it again," said Anya. "A little more oomph this time, kids," Simon said, and Anya added, "Bobby, stay turned about fifteen degrees to your left. I could see the handle before it was supposed to be there."

One of the makeup girls swabbed the blood from Bobby's chin and handed him another blood capsule.

Anya called, "Action."

Three more tries, and Schiff was satisfied.

"Bring the camera back in." Smith heaved a sigh of relief. Simon waded out into the water to stand beside Janine. I couldn't hear him because he spoke so low, but his gestures told me he was telling her how to stab the killer.

"Places." Bobby hovered over the water, ready to fall forward. "Action." Bobby took a breath and went face down in the water, the knife sticking up like an antenna.

The ghastly face of the lake-thing split into a hideous grin. Janine screamed as the claw-like hands reached for her over Bobby's floating corpse. Her face shifted from fear to anger and she grabbed the handle of the knife. "Cut." Janine tapped Bobby on the shoulder and he came up for air.

It took three takes to get the combination of expression and movement that Schiff wanted from his players. Then Bobby and Dick Hunter, who played the Lake Thing got out of the water while Barlow and one of his helpers dragged a mannequin that was a dead ringer for Hunter's character into the lake.

"Action."

Janine held the knife with both hands over her head and drove it into the chest of the Lake Thing mannequin, screaming, this time in pure rage. She kept screaming as she pulled it out and drove it in again and again. I suspect that Schiff told her to do it that way the better to show off her breasts for the camera.

The Lake Thing fell backward and lay, floating in the moonlight while Janine stood, gasping from the exertion, her breasts heaving. That would play well with the pre-pubescent boys and the ball-cap beer-belly crowd.

"Cut. One more to be safe. Good job, DiBasil. I could see real anger there."

I'm no shrink, but I suspect that the killer dummy was Janine's surrogate for Schiff. Schiff got his "one more time" and two more after that before Anya finally called, "That's a wrap for tonight. Pack it up."

As if on cue, almost everybody on the set lit up, most of them cigarettes, though an occasional sniff of grass wafted by. Then the logistical ballet began anew as everyone picked up his or her assigned piece of the gear and headed toward the cabins.

I said to Shultz, "Is that a ritual, you know, like smoking after sex?"

"Nobody's allowed to smoke while we're filming," he said around his own cigarette. "The smoke has an inconvenient habit of drifting into the frame. It really doesn't matter when they're running the fog machine, but Simon insists nobody smoke anyway. Loose smoke is something he can't control."

Shultz shook a cigarette halfway out of the pack and offered it to me.

"No, thanks. I quit a long time ago."

He nodded. "That was a good trick you used to fix the cable."

"It works," I said, "and it's a lot quicker than trying to solder those thin wires, but we probably won't be able to do it too many more years. The refills in most ball points these days are plastic, not brass, if they have refills at all, Bic pens, for example."

Leighty came up behind us. "Sam?" We turned and saw him standing, for the first time all night, without his clipboard. He looked as naked as Janine and Bobby without it.

"Simon was pleased at what you did, fixing the mic cable. You saved us time and money. He wants you on the payroll and he wants you here every day."

Shultz gave us a two-finger salute. "I'll leave you two to sort out the particulars. Thanks, Sam."

"What's that involve?" I said to Leighty.

"Be here every day while we shoot."

"And night?"

"And night."

"Ed, I have other commitments. I'm booked to play a couple of nights a week. And if I'm here, when will I write the score for this epic?"

"Well," he hesitated. "Simon thought you could move your operation to one of the cabins."

"Uh-uh." I shook my head. "No deal, Ed. I need my own space to work. I'll come every day or night that I can, but my schedule is my own. Tell Simon he can pay me *per diem* when I show up."

Leighty gnawed at his lower lip. "I'll see what Simon says." He stood for a moment shuffling his feet. "What did you think about the shoot tonight?" I got the impression that he was about as interested in my opinion as he was the price of soybeans on the Commodities Market, but he was malingering to postpone delivering unwanted news to the King.

"It's not Kurosawa, but I can see it would entertain enough people to make a profit. I read once that two of the signs of a decaying civilization are preoccupations with violence and the occult. Nobody's going to go broke this month pandering to either one."

Leighty pushed out his lips, nodded his head, and walked away without another word.

"**Y**ou turned down a contract to work on the set?" Jenny took the news wide-eyed. She was standing in front of the bathroom mirror in her pink waitress uniform brushing her hair. "Oh, Sam." She shook her head in disbelief.

When I first told her I'd be working on a film, she was ecstatic. She'd always wanted to be in movies. "It's not all it's cracked up to be, Jen. Ninety-nine percent of the people I saw working out there were grunts and donkey labor."

"Still, it would be fun to be on a movie set." She ran the brush through her long red hair

"I'll check with the site manager. Maybe you can come with me sometime and see how it's done."

"Ooh, I'd like that." Jenny smiled and that Glenn Close gap between her front teeth got to me like it always does. Jenny moved in with me six months after the Danny Barton incident, and we get along about as well as any two people sharing the same space. The fifteen years' difference in our ages doesn't bother either one of us.

"Maybe I could be an extra or something," she said, a hopeful tone in her voice.

"I read the script, and it's basically eight principals in a remote wooded location. I didn't see any scenes with extras, but they may change the script at some point and need more people. This isn't like Schiff's last movie, *Tree Walkers*, with fifty or so volunteers staggering around with leaves in their hair and tree branches growing out of their skulls."

She pulled a moue. "Damn, and I thought I'd be discovered."

I put my arms around her waist and buried my face in her thick red hair. "Darlin', you've already been discovered."

Jenny laughed and twisted out of my grip. "Later, Mozart. Dora's starts serving breakfast in forty minutes. Gotta go."

She pulled her hair back into a pony tail. That always disappointed me for some reason; maybe that hair swinging free made me think of Jenny's spirit, and I hated to see it restrained in any way. She stood on tiptoes and kissed me then slid away before I could get my arms around her again. "Get good things done, Sam. I'll see you later." Then she was out the door and gone.

And there I was, alone with a blank slate of a day ahead of me. I couldn't work on the scene from last night until Leighty brought the video, so I decided to catch up with the other strings attached to my life.

There was an e-mail from Denny Martini, the English Department Chairman at HACC. He said that said he was disappointed that I couldn't teach my usual comp section over the summer, but he understood and wished me success on the film project. Since my album *Requiem* made the charts last year, I haven't been so needy of the adjunct teaching paycheck, but I'm not ready to burn that bridge yet.

Another e-mail was a request from the research paper mill that paid me to write essays for lazy rich kids. They wanted a ten-pager on William Faulkner's novel *Absalom, Absalom*. I thought it over; it would be fun to suggest that David Milch derived his *Deadwood* character Al Swearingen from Faulkner's Thomas Sutpen, but I decided to pass on that one. I've always said that if Faulkner wrote Westerns, they'd read like *Deadwood*, but I figured I'd need the time to work on the film score.

The third I opened was from an old friend, Ricky Stover. Like me, Ricky was a veteran of the music life, almost my age, and still making a living with a guitar under his arm. He spent his winters between the ski resorts in the Northeast and the cruise ships out of Miami and his summers at the beaches. His forte was playing solo and playing every request the crowd threw at him.

"Sam, I got a problem," the message read. "I'm booked the whole month of June five nights a week at Rollo's in Myrtle Beach, and my doctor scheduled me for surgery June second. I don't want to lose the gig, and my contract says I can substitute an act of 'equal or greater talent' if I can't make it. Can you help me out and do four nights that week?"

Ricky was one of the few people I knew these days who still ran his whole musical career without an agent. He managed all his own booking, taxes, and promotion. The substitution clause in his contracts was a smart idea, and typical of his experienced management style.

I was about to type a regrets message as a reply when the doorbell rang. Through the peephole, I saw Ed Leighty, his canoe of a nose exaggerated by the fish eye lens. People don't realize it, but when they stand too close to a peephole, they look like something in a funhouse mirror.

I opened the door and Leighty handed me a manila envelope. "Here's a DVD of last night's footage and some pages of script changes. We'll start shooting at four to catch the late afternoon sun."

"Okay. Is it all right if I bring my girlfriend Jenny with me?"

"Sure. It isn't a closed set. They're pitching tents and playing volleyball; that kind of shit today. As long as she stays back out of the way, it shouldn't be a problem."

"Fair enough. You want to come in, have some coffee?"

Leighty shook his head. "I have a 'to-do' list from Simon you wouldn't believe, starting with replacing that mic cable you patched up last night."

"I'd try Malone's Music over on Fourth. Tell Johnny, the owner I sent you over. He's got two of everything where sound's concerned."

"Thanks for the tip." Ed looked past me into the apartment. "I can see why you'd rather work here than in one of the cabins."

"All the comforts of home. I've been on the road before. It gets old living out of a suitcase."

"I'm used to it. Actually, I've been doing it so long, I feel odd when I spend a week in my apartment in L.A."

I held up the envelope. "I'll get on this right away."

"Thanks, Sam. I'll see you this afternoon."

In the envelope I found the DVD in a paper sleeve. The disc had a printed label that said "Property of Last Light Productions, unauthorized reproduction is strictly prohibited"; blah, blah, blah. Written in blanks were the working title of the film, the scene list, and the date.

I popped the DVD into the player and sat on the couch. A yellow screen appeared on the TV and the same legal boilerplate scrolled bottom-up. Then abruptly the forest clearing appeared. The scene was familiar, but looked totally different from what I saw with my own eyes. Maybe it was the lighting and the contrast. Unlike the human eye, the camera doesn't open its iris unless you tell it to. The unchanging look as Lianna moved from moonlight into partial darkness was unsettling, as if subconsciously I was telling my eyes to adjust and they refused.

There came the arms, the face, and the knife. I watched it again. One minute fifty-eight seconds. I looked at the array of instruments hanging on my living room wall and settled on my old Martin D-18. Experience has taught me that new music makes more sense on an acoustic guitar the first time around.

I put the scene on a loop and started picking staccato riffs on the muted lower strings. I stayed off the straight major scale, using tritones—the "Devil's interval"—and flat ninths. When moving string to string sounded too linear, I tried cross-picking, skipping first one string then two at a time, then three.

After a dozen passes I had a pretty good riff going. I tried it in different keys then in different octaves. Before I could forget how it went, I set my hand held recorder on the coffee table and pushed the red button.

I recorded the riff before I hung the Martin back on the wall and shut off the DVD player. Let it sit for an hour or so while I went to the gym, then I'd come back to it fresh. I'd have enough time to work it up in a rough form for Simon before I rode out to Tuscarora. Jenny would be back by then, and she could go with me.

I looked back at the computer and decided that e-mailing Ricky could wait an hour, and I grabbed my gym bag and headed out the door.

I set my hand held recorder on the coffee table and pushed the red button.

The Pumphouse is a physical and psychological retreat for me. It's a coed gym, but most of the people in the weight room are men. No matter what was bothering me or how badly, when I went in there to work with the free weights, it all got put on hold for an hour.

Brian, the owner, came over when he saw me signing in at the desk. Brian is my height, or would be if he had hair, but almost half again as wide—all muscle. "Hey, Sam," he waved me over. "Some guy came in from that film company that's making the horror film out at Tuscarora. They were asking about a group rate for the month they'll be here. They said you were working with them."

"Yeah, Last Light Productions."

"Are they reliable, or are they fly-by-nighters?"

"The check they wrote me didn't bounce, if that's what you're worried about. I looked them up on line. They have a track record for success at making trashy, scary movies."

"Well, I guess I'll make them a deal then."

I laughed. "Just don't shoot me if they stiff you."

"Can't stiff me if I make them pay me up front." He grinned. "But you're right; I would shoot you."

Thursdays are usually my leg days, heavy squats with a barbell across my shoulders. Hard physical exercise combined with the clank of the weights and the animal grunts of the lifters always vacuums out my brain and reboots my thinking.

A heavy leg routine followed by light upper body work had me sweating rings under the arms of the "Grammar Cop" T-shirt Jenny gave me for my last birthday. Besides wielding a sharp pen on her papers, I had started proofreading manuscripts for a press in Denver. Another stream of small money, but as long as there are writers, they'll need proofreaders.

Recently, Denny Martini sent around a memo suggesting that instructors use some color other than red when they mark student papers because red ink "sends a negative message" and "disturbs the student." That's the whole point, isn't it—to let the student know that his paper is bleeding and needs triage. I compromised. Instead of red, I now use deep purple, violent without the N, so the paper looks bruised instead. But I'm not totally insensitive; I used hot pink for Breast Cancer Awareness month.

I made an addition to my usual workout a few months before, an exercise that involved straddling the bench with a forty-pound dumbbell in each hand at shoulder height. Twist left and raise the right dumbbell full reach, twisting the wrist and forearm to turn the weight parallel to your trunk. Reverse sides and do the same move. Fifty of those really wind your spring. That was enough. Time to hit the shower.

I carry a bag to the gym, although Brian allows me to keep a locker for myself at the Pumphouse. The regular customers have to take their locks and their gear with them day to day. The locker comes in handy for storing things I don't want to keep in my apartment, like a small stash of hundred dollar bills and Jenny's Christmas presents. She did wonder, though, why her sexy pajamas from Victoria's Secret smelled like my old tennis shoes.

As I shaved, I saw more grey in my beard than I'd noticed before. But then again, I could just as easily be dead. Getting old sucks, but death is the ultimate vacuum.

Just ask Eddie Shay, my old band mate from Gin Sing and Danny Barton who killed him and my friend Lottie Williams, and who would have killed me if I hadn't shot him first. It's been a while since that all came down, and there are nights when I wake up in a cold sweat thinking about how easily it could have gone the other way.

Most criminologists agree that the majority of murders happen over sex, money, and drugs. What drove Danny to kill Eddie and Lottie was ego. Danny was about to be pushed off the tenuous pinnacle of fame, and he wasn't going without a fight. He killed Eddie because Eddie was going solo and could make it; Danny realized that he couldn't go it alone. So he killed Eddie, stole his song, and rode the publicity into an album deal that would have set him up for life. Then Lottie figured it out, tried to squeeze Danny, and he killed her too.

Then I figured it out, and my aim was better than his, not to mention my luck. But for the second time in my life I realized that it was kill or be killed, and I made the right choice.

As soon as I got back to my apartment, the movie project popped into my head again, and I played back the riff I worked up earlier. By itself, it was effective, but it needed more. I pulled an old Fender bass off the wall and plugged it into the computer interface.

I recorded a steady pulse of quarter notes, a monotone, for thirty seconds, then I brought it up in Adobe Audition and opened the Delay Effects. I tinkered with the slap back echo until it made the bass pulse approximate a heartbeat. My natural tendency as a musician was to space the echo so that it fit into the music timing, but with a little cutting and pasting, I had something that was just skewed enough to unsettle the listener. Speed it up at the right moments and abruptly stop it when Lianna leans against the tree, then high speed when she sees the hand and stop it cold for the knife thrust.

I skipped lunch and by three o'clock, I had a workable rough cut to play for Simon. Not bad, I thought, although I knew in my heart he'd find some way to put his fingers in it.

Jenny came home after her shift. "Get changed. I'm taking you on a dream date."

She cocked her head and gave me her skeptical one-eyed stare. "Where are we going?"

"Camp Tuscarora. I'm taking you to the shoot."

"Oh, God, I'm, a mess. I'll have to take a shower, wash my hair…"

"No time, darlin'. Just change your clothes, and make it fast. I have to be there by four. We'll be out in the woods, so wear something outdoorsy."

A half an hour later, we were in my old red Caravan heading for Tuscarora. I had my sound track demo burned with the video onto a DVD. I try to keep up with the software, but when I find something that works for me, I usually stick with it. That's the case with Magix. The software package was originally designed to make music videos, but it does pretty well for soundtrack work. Some new software apps have come out in recent years, but I don't have the time or ambition to tackle a steep learning curve.

The camp was busy when we pulled in. I shut off the motor and Jenny flipped the sunshade down for a quick look at her hair and makeup.

"Come on, Jen; we aren't going to meet the Queen of England."

She stuck her tongue out at me and laughed. "I just want you to be proud of me, and I want those trampy little starlets to see what you've got at home."

"One look at you and they'll all surrender."

A few people were on the porch of one of the cabins working on the Lake Thing costume. They told us the shoot was out in the woods and to follow the signs. We followed arrows spray painted on cardboard with hunter's orange and nailed to trees till we reached a clearing about a half mile from the camp. The crew was busy setting up one of a pair of tents.

"Sam!"Anya Savage hurried over. "Good that you're here. We have a problem. Tom Marshall, the actor who was supposed to play the Sheriff's deputy can't be here. He was driving from Cleveland and he's stuck in gridlock; some accident on the Ohio Turnpike."

"And?"

"We need somebody to play the deputy. We have the uniform and the cowboy hat for you. You're the right age, and if you shave off some of your beard…"

"Whoa, whoa, whoa. Shave my beard?"

"Simon thought if you left the moustache, sort of a Sam Elliot look, it would work."

"I don't know about this. I haven't acted since the Shakespeare Club in college."

"We really need you, Sam. It'll screw up the whole shoot if you don't do it. It'll put us behind schedule."

"Go on, Sam. You can do it." Jenny was more excited than she should have been.

"I'll try, but I'm not shaving anything."

The deputy uniform was a little large, sized for somebody taller and rangier than I am, but we solved the problem by rolling the sleeves up to the elbow and pinning the trouser cuffs. They'd shoot me from the knees up only—the magic of Hollywood.

As the wardrobe girl, a petite little thing named Claryce—doesn't anybody name a girl Mary, or Pamela, or Susan anymore?—pinned up the cuffs, I said, "Does this sort of thing happen often?"

She spoke around the pins between her lips, "Only four or five times a day. This is an indie film."

Like most things in life, working on a film was a lot of "hurry up and wait." Once I was ready, I stood around for about two hours while the four leads struggled with putting up the second tent. While they were doing that I went over my lines. Jenny read Janine's and Bobby's parts.

The scene involved my throwing open the flap of their tent while they were writhing naked in a double sleeping bag—another excuse to show off Janine's attributes, I guess.

The makeup girls were combing something through my beard to make it a little darker when Simon strolled over. "You're not shaving?"

I grinned. "Not for you, not for the Pope, and not for Jesus Christ Superstar."

He shrugged. "I guess under the circumstances, beggars can't be choosers, right, Dunne?" Then he noticed Jenny. "Who are you?"

I answered him before she could. "This is my girlfriend, Jenny Alton."

Simon ignored me and walked all around Jenny like he was studying a sculpture. "Yes. Yes." He took her by the elbow. "Come with me, please," a request, not a command. "Savage. Get DiBasil over here."

Anya came in a moment with Janine in tow. Janine was wearing sweats and a bored look. Simon turned to her. "Would you stand beside Jenny, please?"

Janine stood beside her and Simon was silent for a moment his right hand over his chin and his mouth, a contemplative pose. "DiBasil, take off your top." She did. Jenny's eyes widened at the sight of Janine's breasts, but she didn't say anything. Simon turned to her and said. Now, Jenny, would you remove yours, please."

"Wait a minute, Simon," I said, and he held up a pre-emptive hand, otherwise ignoring me.

"Indulge me."

He turned back to Jenny. "Please."

Jenny looked at me and then back at Simon. She unbuttoned her blouse, hesitantly at first, then resolvedly as if she'd made some major decision. She pulled her arms out of the sleeves and held it at her side. I was glad she wore a brassiere.

"Do you see it, Savage?"

"Yeah." Anya walked around the pair of women. "It's amazing,"

"What are you talking about?" I demanded.

"Your girlfriend is almost a perfect match with Janine. A body double."

"We could put her in a wig for distance shots."

Simon shook his head. "No, that wouldn't do. Jenny, would you be willing to dye your hair black?"

Jenny didn't have to say yes or even nod. By the look on her face, I realized that the manipulative son of a bitch had won.

The young lovers are locked in a passionate embrace, their mouths searching, tasting, nibbling at each other. Silhouetted against the wall of the tent, she roughly pushes him by the shoulder onto his back and straddles him. She starts rocking back and forth, her breasts swinging like ripe fruit on a wind-blown branch. Faster. Her breath becomes ragged and she arches her back.

"Cut. Move the camera to the other side of the tent." The crew hustled to move the equipment. "I want to get a third angle too, so that we can cross fade them into each other," Simon said to Anya. It seemed almost comical, him giving her orders: she was half a head taller the he was and judging by the shoulders on her, she could have knocked him on his ass with little effort. Simon peered at the small digital display on the camera. "The light's too harsh, Savage. Tone it down."

One of the techs held the white balance board beside Janine. She yawned. "How many more takes do you need, Simon?"

"As many as necessary for me to get what I want. Let's try it on top of the sleeping bag."

"What are we making, a goddamned stag film?"

"No, we're making money, DiBasil, you included."

Behind Simon, standing off to the side, I saw a small, spare woman wearing a maroon pants suit and glasses on a chain around her neck. I couldn't see her face clearly at that distance, but I could see her well enough to know she wasn't amused at what she was watching. I nudged Graham. "Who's the Republican?"

"That's Elizabeth Stout. She's Simon's wife."

"He's married?" Jenny said.

"For about two years now."

"They look like the original Odd Couple," I said.

"You have no idea."

"Action."

When they shot from the other side of the tent, we couldn't see inside, but our side of the tent was open now and I got an eyeful. Hooray for Hollywood. Jenny elbowed me and whispered, "Don't enjoy it so much." Guilty as charged, but it was at that moment I realized the reason I found Janine so sexy was her uncanny resemblance—at least from the neck down—to Jen. Convincing Jenny of that would be a hard sell, though.

"'My strength is as the strength of ten because my heart is pure'—Tennyson."

"'Bull. Shit.'—Henry Miller."

Savage came over. "Okay, Sam, you're up." I put the campaign hat on my head and felt like Smokey the Bear.

My scene involved opening the flap of the tent and peering inside with a little more than professional interest, which didn't call for much acting on my part. Anya framed it from the outside after an over-the-shoulder viewpoint shot approaching the tent and my hand reaching to throw back the flap. Four takes and that was done.

Janine was facing away from the entrance so that she gave the camera a three-sixty show as she turned around to confront the intruder. They shot that bit a few times then moved the camera inside to shoot me head on looking into the tent.

"Action."

"I was going to ask if you folks were all right, but from the looks of things, I guess you are." The line seemed stupid to me, but I was in no position to ad-lib.

"Cut." Simon said. "Do it again. Dunne, can you give me a little drawl? This is supposed to be West Virginia. You sound like South Philly."

"Ah'll see what I kin do fer ya."

Simon rolled his eyes. "Not quite so far south, okay? And leer when you say it."

I shrugged and looked over to Jenny. She grinned and gave me a thumbs-up.

"And action."

Two more tries and Simon was satisfied.

The next scene was the tent interior shot from the outside. "Action."

Janine pulled a corner of the sleeping bag over herself and Bobby sat up.

"What's the matter with you, man?" Bobby said. "Didn't you ever hear of privacy?"

"Since you brought that up, this is private property. Do you have permission from the owner to be here?"

"We aren't hurting anything. What's the big deal?"

"This isn't the safest place for a picnic, son. What if I was a serial killer?" I almost said "were." It's the English professor in me.

"How do we know you aren't?" Janine said, radiating anger like a Franklin stove. She was good.

"You don't," I said, "and that kinda makes my point for me, doesn't it? It's two hours till dark. I'd suggest you and your friends pack up and go find yourselves a motel room. Have a nice day." I let the flap down as Janine said, "Asshole."

And so it went for five more takes as they shot the same scene from inside the tent, behind me, and beside me. It was like recording for an LP. Play the same song or solo over and over until you either get it right or have enough good pieces to patch together.

I must have done okay with the accent because Simon didn't mention it again. When we wrapped for supper, Jenny gave me a big hug. "You did a great job."

"Thanks. I really couldn't tell from where I was standing."

"What happens next?"

"What happens next is one of the reasons why the bit players work for sub-minimum wage while they're being discovered. We're about to be fed."

Back at the cabins, the cast and crew were queueing up around a pair of folding tables with a layout of food and drinks. There were piles of boxed sandwiches, each with a deli pickle, cookie, and chips, a row of pour-spout cardboard containers with coffee, tea, and lemonade, and a tub filled with ice; no beer, but lots of Mountain Dew and Red Bull.

When we got closer, I saw Panera Bread wrappers in the trash can at the end of the tables. Ed Leighty was standing beside it.

"You guys get Panera to cater?"

Ed nodded, chewing a bite of sandwich. "Yeah. We use them a lot. I was able to work a deal. Believe it or not, they're cheaper than some of the fast food chains. Besides, the crew gets tired of eating pizza, Big Macs, and Taco Supremes night after night. Grab a sandwich box while you still have a choice: turkey, ham, tuna salad, and Mediterranean veggie. The small boxes on the sandwich table are chicken soup and tomato basil."

"I brought a rough out of the soundtrack music for the tree scene. It's in my van. I'll get it for you after we eat."

Jenny and I each took a sandwich box and sat at one of the picnic tables with Graham and a tall fuzzy kid named Jerry, who was a film student from the Douglas School in a little town near Pittsburgh called Monessen.

"You're really Sam Dunne? The Sam Dunne?" he said, almost as wide-eyed at me as Jenny was at the film set.

Jenny answered for me. "The Dunne and only. Singer-songwriter extraordinaire."

"That's really impressive, man. I have *Requiem* on the playlist in my iPhone. It's really good music."

I smiled modestly. "Thanks for the kind words. Getting on the charts is a lot of 'right place, right time.' The real trick is to do it again, and I haven't done it yet."

"Well, when the next one comes out, I'll buy it." Jerry nodded emphatically.

"What's your specialty, Jerry?" Jenny said.

"Special effects and makeup. It's what I always wanted to do. I've taken seven classes at Douglas from Tom Savini—you know who he is. He supervises the makeup and effects program."

"Oh yeah," I said. "It's hard to forget his work on camera and off in *From Dusk til Dawn*. And *Dawn of the Dead*, and *Creepshow*."

"You know your movies."

"I've been a fan most of my life. Did you do the work on the Lake Thing?"

"Some of it. Marty designed the makeup but I did most of the work on the mannequin."

"Good job."

Anya Savage sat beside Jenny. "Hi, guys. Marcie, Jerry, could you excuse us for a minute?" Which they correctly interpreted, probably from experience, as "get lost." Which they did.

She said to Jenny, "Simon and I talked, and we want to know whether you'd be interested in working as a double for Janine."

Jenny, who's been around me long enough to pick up some of my attitude, said, "Before I say yes or no, what does that involve?"

"You would stand in for Janine while we're setting up shots, be on camera in her place at a distance, and from behind while we set up face scenes and close ups with her. Because she's in so much of the film, it would save us days we need to meet the schedule. We're already a day and a half behind."

"I'll have to take time off my job. What's it pay?"

"That's something for you to negotiate with Simon. But you work early in the day, right?"

"My shift is over at three."

"Maybe we can set things up so you won't miss much work. What are your days off?"

"Sunday and Monday."

"I can juggle some of the shooting schedule to work around that."

Jenny turned to me. "What do you think, Sam?"

"You're a big girl, Jen. It's your call."

"I think it sounds pretty good. I guess I'll have to dye my hair, right?"

"One of our people will do it for you so we're sure it's a good match for Janine." She paused, as if carefully choosing the words for her next sentence. "There's one other thing. You may have to do some scenes partially nude. Is that a problem?" I noticed Anya wasn't specific.

Jenny bit her lip, thinking it over. She looked at me then back at Anya. "No, it's no problem. I'll do it."

After the moon rose, we were back at the lake for the movie's denouement, the scene in which the female mate of the Lake Thing comes out of the water and slashes Janine's throat. It couldn't be shot the night before because alterations had to be made to the Lake Thing costume to make it distinctly female. Marty had altered the face and added one sagging, uncovered dug, and put a long wig and a different set of rags on Dick Hunter. *Voila.* He was now a she.

The lights were set up, the campfire was relit, and Janine, Dick, and Bobby waded out into the lake. Jerry followed, dragging the Lake Thing mannequin into the water with him.

"Christ, the water's cold," Janine said. "It wasn't this cold last night."

Marcie Graham, standing beside Jenny and me, said, "That's okay. It'll make her nipples stand at attention without having to pack them in ice."

"Simon does that?" Jenny looked alarmed.

Graham nodded. "Whatever it takes. We all have to play 'Simon Says.'"

I whispered to Jenny, "Having second thoughts?"

She didn't answer. She just looked straight ahead.

They took the white balance and focused the shot. In the shadow under Janine's chin, Marty had secured a bleeder device that would cascade stage blood, triggered by a radio operated control gadget taped onto Janine's back. When the knife crossed her throat, Janine would bleed. A lot.

"Okay, people," Anya said. "Let's get it right the first time. Places." Bobby poised to go face down in the water. Dick crouched behind Janine. Jerry was up to his chin holding the mannequin of the now dead Lake Thing in place.

"Rolling." Bobby took a huge breath of air and went face first into the lake. "Action."

The girl gasps for breath, then she begins to sob, wracking, heart tearing sobs that shake her whole body. Behind her, the female Lake Thing rises so fast it seems like a magic trick. A misshapen hand grabs the girl's hair and pulls her head back, and before she can scream, draws the gleaming blade of a knife across her throat in a vicious slash.

Blood pours over the girl's breasts, her arms flail, and her eyes bulge.

Something was wrong. Janine fell forward and Dick held onto her hair. Her head went back and I suddenly realized her throat was really cut as the wound opened like a second gaping mouth.

"What the hell?" Simon said.

Jenny screamed. Someone said, "Jesus Christ!"

Anya shouted, "Cut! Cut, goddamnit!" and thrashed out into the water.

Dick stood staring in disbelief, first at the bloody knife, and then at Janine's gory corpse. He let go of her, and she slid into the water, her hair fanning out around her head.

"Help her!"Anya screamed.

It was then I noticed that the camera was still running, Smith in shock, not even looking through the lens.

"Shut it off."

He blinked. "Wha-what?"

"Shut off the fucking camera." I started ripping out cords, figuring one of them was to the power supply. The red light winked out.

"Call 911,"shouted Leighty. "Somebody call 911."

"I think it's a little too late for that, Ed," said Simon, staring at Janine's bobbing corpse.

I pulled out my cell phone and held down the button to turn it on. As I was dialing 911, Simon saw me and ran over. He grabbed my wrist. "Tell them there's been an accident."

I shook him off, probably a little rougher than I needed to. "She's dead!" I snapped at him. "That's what I'll tell them."

While I gave the operator information, some of the crew carried Janine onto the shore and laid her on a blanket by the campfire. Lying on her back closed the wound in her throat and she looked almost as if she were peacefully asleep in the flickering glow of the firelight.

Dick was still standing in the water holding the knife. He pulled off the creature wig and the facial applications with his free hand. Ed came up behind him and put Dick in a bear hug, pinning his arms. Dick didn't resist. Anya reached for the knife.

"Don't touch it," I shouted. Her head jerked around and she looked at me. "Unless you want your fingerprints on it."

I pulled a handkerchief out of my back pocket and waded into the lake. I wrapped the cloth around the knife and gently took it from him.

Ed and Anya walked Dick to the shore, where he collapsed.

"He's in shock," one of the techs said. "Get a blanket over him."

"And while you're at it," Simon said, "Throw one over her too." As Marcie drew the blanket over Janine's corpse, Simon stared at it like a man watching a ship sail, never to return.

The Sheriff's Department arrived with an ambulance, too late for Janine, but useful for Dick. I'm no expert on law enforcement, but I think Sheriff Billings was out of his depth. He didn't seem to know quite what to do with the crime scene. I didn't say a word. I learned a long time ago when around cops, the best thing to do is keep your mouth shut.

A deputy took statements and another one took photos while Billings had a long conference with Simon and Anya.

The night dragged on, but we weren't allowed to leave. It was almost three when I heard a voice say, "Just like old times, huh, Sam?"

Mike Kearny, Hanniston PD's chief homicide detective was walking in my direction alongside his partner Devon Wilson. Salt and Pepper, the Hanniston cops called the pair. Kearny was tall and rangy, a tousled head of sandy hair sticking out in odd places from a few well-placed cowlicks. His partner Devon had the darkest skin I'd ever seen on a black man, and a shaved head that shone in the halogen crime scene lights. If Kearny was NBA, Wilson was NFL, with enough muscle for two of me.

"Where's your necktie?" Kearny was famous for wearing the same Salvation Army clip-on tie with all his JC Penney rack suits.

"Out of uniform." Kearny grinned. Devon looked as if he just stepped out of a *GQ* ad, suit, shirt, and tie immaculate.

"When are you going to teach Columbo here how to dress, Devon?" Wilson accented the first syllable of his name with a long E.

Devon laughed. "Why do that? He makes me look even better than I am already."

"What are you two doing out here?"

"Heard there were fresh donuts in the catering truck." Devon grinned. "I like the pink ones with the sprinkles."

"I thought this was the Sheriff's jurisdiction. He seems to have everything pretty well in hand."

Kearny snorted. "He does now. He was smart enough to request our highly professional assistance. Tom's okay with deer poachers and pot growers, but there are some things Barney Fife just can't handle by himself."

"I'll vote for that," I said. Kearny and I had a history. He was the lead detective in Eddie Shay's murder, and for a while he had me pegged as the prime suspect. It was Kearny who asked me the now famous question: Do you really think you could kill somebody? I say famous because it showed up in Wendy Conn's book about the murder, *Dead Man's Melody*, and went viral on social media for about ten minutes. Andy Warhol was an optimist.

Kearny said, "I'm guessing you're the most responsible adult in this bunch, Sam, and I admit, that is a stretch, but tell me, what the hell happened here?"

"They were shooting a scene for the movie, and from what I understand, Dick—Dick Hunter—was supposed to fake killing Janine DiBasil with a dull knife. She had blood packs and all the other stuff on her to make it look real. But when they ran the scene, Dick used a real knife, and he actually cut her throat with it."

"Do you think he did it on purpose?" Kearny looked around as he spoke as if the killer would suddenly light up and he might miss it.

"Not that I could see. He was genuinely stunned at the whole business. He was in shock."

"So somebody switched the knife?"

"You mean intentionally?"

"Yeah, for the sake of argument."

"I suppose that's possible, but it could just as easily have been an accident." I shrugged. "Somebody picked up the wrong knife off the prop table."

Devon shook his head. "Don't they have some kind of quality control around here to prevent shit like that?"

"This ain't MGM, Devon," Kearny said. "What about insurance?"

"Beats me. I just started here two days ago. You'll have to talk to the people in charge about that."

"So exactly how did this Dick Hunter slash her?"

"You can watch it for yourself. It's all in the camera."

Kearny's eyes widened. "Oh yeah? Billings didn't tell me that."

It suddenly occurred to me that maybe he didn't know because Simon didn't tell him.

"Stick around, Sam," Kearny said. "We'll be right back." He and Devon headed to the cabin where the deputies were standing around.

"Uh oh," I said to Jenny.

"What?"

"I think I just caused a problem."

"So exactly how did this Dick Hunter slash her?"

#

It was four o'clock when Kearny finally turned everybody loose, although Jenny and I were the only people who left the place. Everyone else was staying at the camp. The coroner had come for Janine's body and Dick Hunter was in the hospital handcuffed to his bed with a uniform outside the door. Poor bastard, I thought, from what I could see, he was the last person on the planet who'd want to kill Janine.

Kearny's question came back to me: Do you really think you could kill somebody? If he asked Dick Hunter the day before, Hunter would have said no. If you asked him now, he'd probably still give the same answer.

Simon was in a major bind. Kearny impounded the rented camera as evidence. The scene with Janine's death was only one file on the data card. Everything they had shot that day, including my scene as the deputy was now downtown in the evidence locker. When I left, Simon was on the phone to the execs at Screamer Pictures and still talking in his same soft voice.

"Do you think they'll shut down the picture, Sam?" Jenny's face glowed in the dashboard lights.

"Probably. I can't see how they could continue without their star. They could put a mask on just about anybody to replace Dick, but they can't do that with Janine. I guess it depends on how much they filmed before today. I probably shot myself in the foot on this one. If they shut down the picture, I lose my job. If they don't, I'll probably be fired anyway. Simon'll blame me for the camera being seized."

"Wouldn't Kearny have taken it anyway?"

"Sooner or later, but Simon would have had a chance to download the data card. Then he'd have the other scenes to edit and work with."

"Well, whatever happens, it's out of your reach now."

"I wish I hadn't turned down the summer class. Maybe Dennis hasn't filled the slot yet. I'll e-mail him in the morning."

"It's already morning. I have to be at work in two hours. I'm going to get a shower and change, then go in early. Two or three cups of Dora's coffee will keep me rolling, but when I get home this afternoon, don't stand between me and the bed."

I e-mailed Dennis and crossed my fingers. Then I thought about Ricky's gig in Myrtle Beach. One or the other might salvage my finances after all.

I looked at the clock. Eight forty-seven. I speed dialed Joe Mancini, my agent. I figured I'd wake him up for a change.

I'd enjoyed a wave of small venue shows and college concerts while *Requiem* was hot, but demand, like fame, was fleeting. I was a notch higher on the ladder, but only one. I was back to doing a lot of resort work and some one-nighters in the better-paying clubs. Joe did his best, but an old horse is a tough sell.

"Sam." Wide awake. "What's got you out of bed so early?"

"Haven't been there yet. Got some bad news about the movie gig."

Joe didn't say a word through the whole story of the night before. When I finished, he said, "You always did have the touch, Sam."

"Now the good news, maybe. You didn't book anything for me the first week of June, did you?"

"No, you said you'd need the time to work on the soundtrack."

"Good. Got an e-mail from Ricky Stover. He wants me to do a fill-in at Rollo's in Myrtle Beach that week."

"Myrtle Beach ain't what it used to be where live music's concerned, Sam, but most places aren't. Rollo's is still a pretty good venue, though. What's the payout?"

"Don't know. I'd be subcontracting to him."

"So he's still running his own show, huh?"

"Yep. Give him a call and see if you two can meet in the middle."

"I'll see what I can work out."

I gave Joe the contact info and decided sleep was more important than food. I was asleep less than an hour when the phone rang.

"Sam? It's Ed Leighty."

"Yeah? What?"

"How well do you know this cop Kearny? I heard him call you by your first name."

"I'm not on his Christmas card list. Why?"

"Simon wants to know if you can get him to release the camera and the footage on it. It's a rental, and it costs us every minute whether we use it or not." They were sly. Don't even mention the fact that it's my fault the camera was impounded, but instead, offer me a chance to redeem myself.

"It's evidence in a homicide, Ed."

"We can give them that footage and take back the rest. We need the camera so we can start shooting again, and we need the other scenes so we can edit them."

"Are you joking?" I was suddenly wide awake. "That girl isn't even cold yet and you people are ready to yell 'Action!' Jesus."

"We work, you, work, buddy." Another carrot with a stick tied to it. Get the camera back or my paycheck evaporates and yours, too.

It was against my better judgment, but I said, "Okay, I'll talk to Kearny, but I can't promise anything. Kearny likes me about as much as he likes a toothache."

Leighty hung up, his duty discharged.

I figured I'd do better with Kearny after I had a few more hours of sleep. No logic there, but it still seemed like a good idea.

I woke up just before Jenny came home from her shift at the diner. I put in a call to the police station, but Kearny was out. Probably out cold, I thought; his night was longer than mine. I left my cell phone number and asked for a call back.

In five minutes, I had the coffee going and two pieces of bread in the toaster. Jenny had me eating healthful whole-grain bread for a while, but a round of gout in my big toe led me to the doctor. The diet he gave me said whole grains were a no-no, along with shrimp, scallops, and nuts. So, I went back to white bread and peanut butter for breakfast.

I suppose Jenny has good intentions when she tells me, "eat this, not that; do this, not that." But I've come to the conclusion that if I follow everyone's advice, I might live an extra fifteen minutes, and that will be tacked onto the end of my life when I'm ninety-seven and wish I were dead anyway. And in that fifteen minutes, I don't think I'll find the solution to world peace or a cure for cancer, so I pretty much do whatever the hell I want.

I sat down on the sofa and reached for the remote control. It was a little after three, and the local news wouldn't be on until five. I switched to cable news, and in a few minutes, there it was. "Murder on the Set" was the title across the bottom of the screen. A very serious young man with extraordinarily white teeth and a windbreaker with the network logo over his heart stood at the camp entrance with the Camp Tuscarora sign over his shoulder. A Marks County Sheriff's Department cruiser, red and blue strobing like a cheap light show, blocked the road.

He took sixty seconds to say essentially nothing except that details of the death of actress Janine DiBasil were "sketchy," but he would keep the viewer informed "as things unfold." Then for two minutes they ran some back story. A studio newscaster talked over clips of ultra violent scenes from other Simon Schiff movies; chainsaws, axes, meat cleavers, and blood, usually dripping from some desperate young woman, the blur bar over her breasts and buttocks. This was followed by thirty seconds of a feminist commentator slamming Simon for his films' depiction of the abuse and torture of women.

Then they ran footage of Simon in the company of two Sheriff's deputies being escorted through a throng of reporters. Anya Savage did her best to stay between him and the cameras, saying, "We will have a statement for the press later today. We have no further comment at this time."

The footage made it look as if Simon were being arrested, when actually, the cops were taking him to the morgue to officially identify Janine's body and sign some paperwork. Behind the police car, off to the side, I saw Elizabeth Stout. It struck me as odd that she'd stand away, not support him in this moment of crisis. She stood, the same expression of displeasure on her face as the one I'd seen earlier in the day, with her hands thrust into the pockets of her jacket.

The apartment phone rang. I hesitated to pick it up when I didn't recognize the number on the caller I.D., but curiosity got the better of me.

"Hi, Sam. It's Wendy."

The appropriate window for a cute remark slipped past before I sorted out my surprise and annoyance. Instead of "Wendy who?" I said, "You're slipping. Last time somebody got killed, you were calling me at seven in the morning. Talk to Kearny yet?"

"He was first on my list, and when he told me you were on the scene, it felt like a class reunion."

Wendy Conn, former reporter for the *Hanniston Sentinel,* now the best-selling author of *Dead Man's Melody,* the story of the Danny Barton case. I can't blame her for being opportunistic and cashing in. After all, it was her story as much as it was mine; we worked together to figure it all out and trap Danny. Even though I came out less than heroic in her version of the story, we did okay, if you overlook the fact that he damn near killed us both and Kearny in the bargain.

The fact that I hadn't heard from her in over a year didn't help my opinion of her, but then again, there were buttons on my phone. Besides, I had Jenny in my life now, so it didn't matter as much as it might have.

"So, Sam, what can you tell me?"

"Is this for print?"

"You now it is."

"I don't know shit, and you can quote me on that."

"Oh, come on, Sam. Kearny told me you saw it happen."

"So did everybody else. Why don't you call one of them?"

"Because they don't have your gift for words, or your pedigree."

"Yeah, I can see the caption now: Sam the Killer talks about the Killer."

She laughed. "That's what I'm talking about. Something quotable."

At that moment, I heard the key turn in the door and Jenny came in.

"I really don't have anything to say about it." I hung up. Jenny stared at me. "Wendy Conn," I said with a shrug. Why lie about it?

She rolled her eyes. "She didn't waste any time, did she? What a vulture."

"I do my thing, you do yours, she does hers," I said. "That doesn't mean any of us has to cooperate with the other."

"I still wish she'd lose your phone number."

"I'll be charitable and write off your attitude to fatigue."

She went into the bedroom and closed the door just a little bit harder than necessary.

Anything between Wendy and me was long gone as far as I was concerned, but Jenny still saw her as a rival for no good reason except that Wendy still breathed. The only reason she'd call me these days was fodder for a story she was writing. Since Janine DiBasil's death made the national news channels, I guess Wendy saw a chance to score with an inside scoop. Well, she wouldn't get it from me.

My cell phone rang again. It was Kearny. "Dunne," he said. "Heard you called."

"Yeah. The folks out at the lake want to know what they have to do to get their camera back."

"Wait; that's all they have to do, just wait."

"It's a rental, Mike. They're paying *per diem* for it. They're on a tight budget. Like you said, this isn't MGM with deep pockets. And they want to have the footage they shot that wasn't involved in the accident."

"That's assuming a lot, isn't it, Sam? An accident?"

"Come on, Mike. You don't really think that kid murdered Janine DiBasil, do you?"

"I'm keeping an open mind. Besides, that's not my call. The D.A. makes that decision."

I could picture Kearny slouched in the chair at his desk wearing one of those polyester suits that ride him like a cardboard box with sleeves, head tilted on the chair back and his feet on a pile of files next to the telephone; the epitome of the public servant.

"Well, at least give me a day when they can have the camera back."

"Autopsy's tomorrow. Can't do much before then." Coroner's inquest is set for a week from today. You talk to our mutual friend?"

"Yeah. She called me, probably right after she called you. You're the go-to guy; I'm the backup."

"I couldn't tell her anything that wasn't already on the news."

"Must've been a short conversation."

"By the way, Sam, I saw the scenes with you at the tent along with the other footage. You make a good Ranger Rick."

I imagined the cops at the station gathered around watching the footage, rewinding at and playing scenes again, freezing frames to study details, and that was before they got to Janine's death. "Listen, Mike, I understand keeping the video card, but you don't need the camera to show it. How about that?"

"Maybe I could get the camera loose, but I need something in return from you."

"Like what?"

"I need eyes and ears on that set. That gang won't talk to me, but they may open up to you, or maybe talk in front of you, give me a handle on the situation."

"They hardly know me. I've only been with them for two days. Besides, I'm no snitch."

"First time for everything. You think it over, and I'll think it over." He snorted. "*per diem*." He hung up.

Most of the trouble I get into is the result of me doing something for somebody else's benefit. You'd think I'd learn, but I never do.

Since that was a dead end, I did what I normally do when I hit the wall: I pick up a guitar and play. A half hour of finger style blues, two bottles of Heineken, and the world didn't seem quite so irritating anymore.

Jenny was in a better mood when she woke up around seven-thirty. I took her out to Mike and Kelli's, a little bar I play regularly as a favor to the owners. Maybe the word for the place isn't "little" so much as "intimate."

When we walked in, I didn't get my usual greeting from Kelli, who always shouts, "Sam I am!" when I walk through the door. Something was up.

We sat on cafe stools at the bar, and in a minute, Mike came over with my Heineken and Jenny's Miller Lite "Hi, Sam. Hi, Jenny."

"You look worried, Mikey," I said. "What's up?"

He looked to either side as if he were going to tell us some state secret. "ASWI was in here last night."

"You mean Asswipe? That's what musicians call them."

ASWI, Affiliated Song Writers International, is a PRO, a performing rights organization. New kids on the block in copyright and royalty enforcement. According to their website, ASWI represents over a hundred thousand copyright holders and goes after the smaller venues the big boys don't bother with. They had been on an enforcement binge in central Pennsylvania the last few months and shut down live music at a half dozen local places.

Their pitch was simple: if you are going to have music in your bar or restaurant, you pay royalty fees that kick back to the copyright holder, sometimes the original composer, sometimes a music publisher, sometimes a record label.

If you ran a smaller establishment like Mike and Kelli's that couldn't afford the tariff, you had two choices: stop running music or hire a lawyer because ASWI was going to haul you into court. Somehow, ASWI missed the irony that stopping venues from running music prevented songs from being heard and lessened their exposure on the market. Less exposure means fewer copies sold, and less money for everyone.

As a songwriter, I understand and respect intellectual property. I don't think people should be cheated out of their just due for a creative product, but we all have to make a living, small business owners included. To strong arm them out of the market, in my eyes, was at best a wrong-headed practice and at worst, a simple shakedown.

"They told me if I wanted to keep running music, I'd have to pay them seventeen hundred dollars a year."

"That's a lot of cash," I said.

"The guys who came in here based that figure on some formula including the square footage of the place, the number of seats at the bar and the number of chairs at the tables."

I nodded. "Standard procedure."

"I don't know what to do. They asked me how often I run live music, since I don't run a DJ, and I told them only on Thursdays when you play here. Then they brought up Half Life, that duo I had in for two weekends a few months ago."

"What did you say about paying the fees?"

"I said I didn't have the money. I said I didn't make the money."

"And they said?"

"They said they'd be back to see me again, and if I wasn't paying up, don't run music."

"Don't sweat it, Mikey. I'll be in Thursday and I'll handle it."

"How?"

"I won't play covers. I'll play all original material, and they can't say shit about it. In the meantime, don't book anybody else until we get this sorted out."

Jenny had a Cajun chicken salad, and I had my favorite from Mike and Kelli's, a Reuben with fries and a dill pickle. I had always helped Mike and Kelli as much as I could, first because they were my friends, and second, because I couldn't find a better Reuben within a hundred miles of Hanniston.

"Why is ASWI picking on Mike and Kelli?"

"They aren't really. ASWI has been combing through this part of Pennsylvania for months and Mike and Kelli just got swept up in the net like every other bar and restaurant owner. The people they ought to go after are the disc jockeys who download all their music free from the internet and pay no royalties. They don't create anything. If anybody's a thief, it's a disc jockey. But the Asswipe enforcers are too lazy to track them down. They go for the stationary targets like Mike and Kelli's, people who are in the same place all the time and have their whole lives and livelihood wrapped up in their business."

Jenny speared a piece of chicken with her fork. "So, when are you running for Congress?"

"Okay," I laughed. "End of sermon."

Mike had the television set over the bar turned on for the daily lottery numbers, and when that was over, the local news came on. I had managed to put Janine's death out of my mind for a while, but the accident led the newscast. Nothing new, but it all came back with a vengeance.

The local news included the press conference Anya Savage set up. She did most of the talking and near the end; Simon read a one-page statement on camera. The general drift was that Janine DiBasil was a talented actress and a good friend to all of the cast and crew and that everyone is shocked and saddened by the tragic accident.

Schiff took no questions, but when a reporter shouted, "does this mean you're going to scrap *Lake Deadly*?" Anya shot back, "That's a decision for the executives at Screamer Pictures to make," and turned her back on the cameras.

"How could they possibly go on with the film after this? Who'd go to see it?"

"P.T. Barnum said that nobody ever went broke underestimating the taste of the American public. There are people out there who'd go to see it *because* someone was killed in the filming, especially a star like Janine."

"That's sick."

"We hate to think about it, Jen, but it's a sick world out there. Like the newsies say, 'If it bleeds, it leads.'"

"Do you think that's how the studio people see it? Is that how Simon sees it?"

I remembered Simon's response to Janine's jibe about making a stag film: "No, we're making money, DiBasil, you included." I figured that pretty well nailed it shut. "My guess is that Simon sees things however the studio tells him to. Drink up and let's go home."

Back at the apartment, I checked my e-mail. Dennis said he was sorry, but he already handed off the summer composition class to another adjunct. No call from Joe Mancini, so I didn't know whether the Myrtle Beach gig was still on the table.

Jenny came out of the bedroom. She'd changed into sweats and pulled her hair back into a ponytail. I sat on the sofa and picked up my copy of *The Collected Stories of Raymond Carver.*

"Is it okay if I put on some music?" Jenny said over her shoulder from the CD case.

"Sure. It won't bother me."

She fussed with the CD player and Santana's version of "Europa" came on. I looked up from my book, eyebrows raised. She turned to me and smiled, and with agonizing slowness, pulled down the zipper of her shirt.

When we were dating, Jenny and I were in my van on our way to the movies when "Europa" came on the radio. She said that as far as she was concerned, that was the "ultimate make out song." We never made it to the movies that night. In fact we never made it out of the van. The song's been a trigger for us ever since.

Jenny came between me and the coffee table and gently took Raymond Carver out of my hands and laid him on the arm of the sofa. She straddled me, and pulled her shirt open. I pulled her to me, nuzzling her breasts and felt myself responding.

There's something darkly erotic about watching someone die, especially in a violent fashion. It makes you aware that you're alive and fills you with the desire to make the most of it. In a few minutes, the song ended and our clothes were scattered on the couch, the coffee table and the floor. One of my socks hung over an arm of the lamp.

"Do you want to go into the bedroom?" I whispered.

She shook her head. "Then we couldn't hear the stereo." She picked up the remote control and clicked it. Then she bent forward over the arm of the sofa.

"Europa" came on again.

When Jenny's right, she's right.

Normally the wheels of justice wouldn't spin so fast, but because the media jumped on Janine's death with both feet, the locals expedited the process. The autopsy was performed, and nothing new was revealed. Janine died from massive hemorrhaging from a severed carotid artery, pure and simple.

Dick Hunter was still in the hospital, nearly catatonic. The meter was running on that one too They'd have to charge him or release him. But release him to what?

The *Sentinel* ran an unsigned editorial talking about "death by stardom" and on the same day ran a front page article liberally quoting a local fire and brimstone minister who denounced Hollywood as Sodom and Gomorrah and filmmakers as "the Devil without horns."

Kearny called me the day after. "So, Sam, you think about what we discussed?"

"I can't help but think you wouldn't be making this offer unless you were already clear to release the camera."

"Have you been out to Tuscarora since the 'accident?'"

"What made you suddenly so charitable? You aren't suspicious anymore?"

"Of course I am. It's my job. I'm a homicide detective, remember?"

"How could I forget?"

"What do you know about Elizabeth Stout, Sam?"

"Simon's wife? Never even met her. She's been on the set every time I was there, but we've never been introduced."

"I hear she's the jealous type."

"Couldn't prove it by me," I said.

"Word is she wasn't too happy with Simon playing Barbie Dolls with the cuties."

"Been talking to Wendy again, huh?" I remembered the look on Elizabeth Stout's face while she watched Simon directing my scene and arranging Janine and the camera for maximum exposure. "You suspect her?"

"You said it yourself: somebody grabbed the wrong knife. What if somebody switched the sharp knife for the dull one to make that happen? We always look at spouses and girlfriends. She had opportunity, and if she was as jealous as people say, she had motive."

"I couldn't comment. I'm not a trained investigator like you."

"But that didn't stop you from going after Danny Barton on your own, did it?"

I let that one slide.

"The offer still stands, Sam. Go hang out at Tuscarora and see what you hear and I'll see about the camera. They don't work, you don't work, right?"

If Kearny wasn't talking to Wendy Conn, he was talking to Ed Leighty. The perversity of knowing things Wendy didn't had a certain appeal. "I'm not wearing a goddamned wire."

"So that's a yes?"

"That's a, 'see what I can do,' kinda like you seeing what you can do about the camera."

"You should've been a lawyer, Sam." He chuckled. "Or maybe a homicide detective."

"Then I'd have to work with the likes of you."

"You already are."

IX

was at the Pumphouse doing an arm routine and left my phone in my locker. I missed two calls. Ed Leighty, the first caller, left a message. The D.A. held a preliminary hearing for Dick Hunter, who was charged with manslaughter. Bail was set at a hundred grand. Ed wanted to know if I could recommend a bail bondsman.

The second call was from Joe Mancini. He didn't leave a message, so I sat in my van in the parking lot and called him back. "Joe? What's the word? You hear from Ricky?"

"No, I heard from your pal Wendy Conn. She asked me for a comment. She's doing a piece for *Nightside* on the 'Sam Dunne Jinx.'"

"The what?"

"'The Sam Dunne Jinx'; you work with Gin Sing, and people die. You work on *Lake Deadly*, and people die. Death seems to follow you around. You're like that guy in *Li'l Abner* with the cloud over his head. That's the drift of her story."

"Maybe I ought to go work with her. Who knows what may happen."

"Oh, Christ, don't say that in front of anyone, or she'll file some bullshit terroristic threat charge against you. What did you do to piss her off?"

"I said no. That's all it takes for her, I guess."

"Well, there's really nothing you or I can do to stop her. You're a public figure and unless she outright libels you, you're fair game for the scandal rags."

It was at that moment that the thought of knowing things Wendy Conn didn't and giving them to somebody else seemed even more appealing. As soon as Joe hung up, I called Kearny.

"I'm in. I'll call you when I hear anything useful. Now, about the camera . . ."

Out at Tuscarora, nothing much was happening when I pulled into the parking lot. Nobody ran out to greet me, or even so much as acknowledge that I was there until I pulled the camera case out of the van. Then Shultz saw the camera and yelled for Simon and Anya, and everybody was happy for at least fifteen minutes.

I pulled Anya aside when the furor died down. "So what's the deal? Is the picture scrapped?"

"The suits at Screamer haven't made a firm decision. I guess they're waiting to see what happens with the charges against Hunter and how big a hit they'll take on the insurance. But in the meantime, Screamer told Simon to edit what footage he has. That's a positive sign."

"So, am I still on the clock?"

"Yeah. If this job shuts down, we can use what you write elsewhere. There'll always be another horror film."

"Funny you put it that way. When a gig folds for me, I say, 'There'll always be another place to play.'"

"To coin a phrase, that's show biz. By the way, we watched the scene with your music. I liked it, and so did Simon, although he said he'd prefer 'less brittle and more slippery,' whatever that means."

"I'm sure he'll tell me, at length."

Anya laughed. "You know him that well already?"

"No, but I know his type. Like you said, 'That's show biz.' I tried to call Ed back about a bondsman, but he didn't answer his cell. What's the word on bail for Dick?"

"He got a guy named Carbone to post the bond."

"Smiling Tony Carboney. I went to high school with him."

"Anyway, that's taken care of and Ed should be bringing Dick back any time now."

At that moment, Simon came out of his cabin and walked over. "They kept the video card, but they made us a copy without the . . . " he hesitated, "accident footage. As soon as we have a few scenes edited, I'll get them to you so you can get back to work on the soundtrack. You also might start thinking about something to use for the opening credits."

Anya broke in. "We will need some music to be playing on the car radio and on the boom box when they're out by the lake in the afternoon. Do you have something we could use for that?"

"You could use a few tracks from *Requiem*, but you'd have to pay the label for them. What if I got you something without strings from a local band I know? Ever hear of Blood Lightning?"

She shook her head. "What do they do?"

"A fusion of rhythm and blues and heavy metal. They're unsigned so far, and I think I could get them for you at a reasonable price."

"Get us a demo, or maybe we could go hear them."

At that moment, Elizabeth Stout came out and joined us. The temperature of the conversation dropped twenty degrees. Her body language excluded Anya from the conversation.

"I just spoke to the Tuscarora manager. They want us out of here immediately. Parents are calling and cancelling their kids' reservations for the summer. He said the management group is worried that our continued presence would, I quote, damage their business posture and deplete their customer base. Bottom line, after the bad press, no parent wants to send a kid here."

Management group? Business posture? I thought. For God's sake. It's a summer camp, not Microsoft. Whatever happened to simplicity?

"So what did you tell him, Stout?" Simon said, seemingly unruffled by the news, as if he expected it all along. I wondered if he called her that at home, say, over the breakfast table or in the sack.

"I told him to read the goddamned contract and read it again. I called Corporate and they're siccing the lawyers on them. I told Tuscarora it would be a pain in the ass to move, and kicked and screamed, but there are lakes all over the state with the same foliage. In the end, we'll probably have to leave before the fifteenth, but if we go into crunch mode, we can get all the location shots wrapped by the time their lawyers kick us out. We leave and save a chunk of the rental fee, plus whatever the legal department can squeeze out of Tuscarora as a penalty for defaulting on the contract."

I realized then that what I thought was the Odd Couple was really a perfectly paired Yin and Yang. Simon was the creative genius and

"I told him to read the goddamned contract and read it again."

Elizabeth was the fiscal pit bull that kept bankruptcy at bay. I also realized that the mean look I saw on her face during the shoot wasn't worn for the occasion. She had furrows in her forehead that botox couldn't touch.

"Wait a minute," I said. "I obviously missed some subtle nuance here. You're going ahead with the film?"

"Sure," Simon said, "All things considered, the press we're getting will ensure that people come to see *Lake Deadly.* You know what they say: no ink is bad ink."

"How will you do that without a star?"

"We were hoping that your girl friend Jenny could take her place."

I usually had a pretty good poker face, but it must have slipped, because Anya jumped in with, "There's really nothing to worry about, Sam. We'll guide her through the process. It's not a Bergman film, you know?"

"She's built like Janine, and with a little Hollywood magic, she can look like her too."

"Corporate approved a CGI component to *Lake Deadly*'s budget," Elizabeth said. My face must have slipped from surprise to confusion. She went on. "Computer Generated Imaging. We'll have the techies replace Jenny's face with Janine's for the dozen or so shots that are up close."

"We'll film additional distance shots to pad the footage that won't require CGI, and add scenes with the other characters to fill out the run time. If things go well, we'll come in on time and not too far over budget."

I was hearing all this but at the same time thinking what ghouls these people were. Janine wasn't even buried yet and they were figuring out ways to capitalize on her death. The monsters weren't in the lake, they were behind the camera.

"Well, you'll have to talk to Jenny about all this," I said. "I can't speak for her."

"We already did, Sam," Anya said. "I talked to her a little while ago. We just wanted to make sure you were on board with the idea."

The real actors, just like the real monsters, were the ones running the shop. This whole conversation was just a *kabuki* dance. The camera iced the cake. I followed a minute of silence with, "So, tell me what you need me to do."

I went home that afternoon and found Jenny at the computer. She stood up when I came in and said, "You heard the news?" Then my face gave me away and she said with less enthusiasm, "You heard the news."

"I won't know how to behave, living with a movie star. It'll take some adjustment."

"No more than me adjusting to life with a rock star."

"What about your job?"

I talked to Dora and Paul. They told me to go for it. They're behind me a hundred percent, but that's not what's most important to me." She put her arms around my neck. "Are you behind me a hundred percent?"

"It's a great opportunity, and I wouldn't dream of holding you back," I hedged.

"But does it bother you, Sam?"

"Not for the obvious reasons. Sure, I hate the thought of half the fourteen-year-olds in America drooling over your boobs, but that's not it. I keep thinking about watching Janine die right in front of me and how I'd feel if it were you instead."

She shuddered. "Yeah. I think about that too, but lightning doesn't strike twice in the same place, right?"

"Not that I've ever heard. What's on the computer?"

"I was reading the copy of the *Lake Deadly* script they sent you. Anya sent me the changes."

"Yeah, I suppose Willis has been busy the past few days."

She kissed me, soft and sensuous. "So, let's celebrate." She slipped out of my arms and tugged me toward the bedroom.

"Don't you want to put on 'Europa' first?'"

She shook her head slowly, and her red hair swung side to side in that sway I've come to find so alluring, like curtains in a summer breeze. "I think we can manage this one all by ourselves."

As we lay tangled in the sheets afterward, I looked over at her red hair fanned out over the pillow and asked myself, will I love her as much when it's dyed black? I decided that yes, I probably would.

Joe called me a few hours later.

"You're on for Myrtle Beach. Four nights at Rollo's. Ricky's a tough negotiator."

I had forgotten about the Myrtle Beach deal in the middle of everything else. I would have slapped my forehead, but I had the phone in one hand and a Heineken in the other. "Well, it looks like the film work will be going on too, but I guess if they need me to do something quickly, they can send it to me."

As I understood it, most soundtrack work was done after the scenes were edited anyway, but Simon had his own style about it all, wanting to put his micromanaging fingers on every detail of production. I thought of the old 50s movie *Thunder Road* about a moonshine war in Tennessee. Robert Mitchum wrote the script, starred in the film, directed the film, wrote the theme song, and even recorded the tune to be released as a 45, although the studio had his co-star Keely Smith sing it over the opening scene. Somehow, her ethereal jazz voice just didn't mesh with the footage, and truth be told, Mitchum's recording would have been a better fit. But I guess if they were paying Keely Smith to be in the film they might as well get their money's worth.

At least Simon didn't cast himself as one of the horny Gen-Xers. He seemed to be more excited about posing people and filming them than being in the scenes; like Kearny said, playing Barbie dolls. And I'm sure that all the outtakes he ever filmed, things a touch too racy for an R rating were on disc in his private library for future reference, to savor in private moments. Orson Welles said, "A Hollywood **studio** is the best toy any kid could ever have." In my opinion, Simon lived up to that aphorism in twisted spades.

Maybe the week in Myrtle Beach would be a blessing in disguise. I'd be out from under Simon and could work up ideas without his constant scrutiny and input. But then there was Jenny to consider. I was hoping she could come with me, but the movie changed all that. She'd have to stay behind, and I wasn't totally comfortable leaving her under Simon's direction. Who knows what that manipulative bastard would try to get away with, bossing around a young, starry-eyed girl instead of a cynical veteran like Janine.

Like it or not, I was stuck with it, but I knew Jenny well enough to trust her judgment. Besides, I'd seen firsthand her ability to say no and stick to it. She'd be okay. I had to believe that.

The next day, we both went out to Tuscarora, Jenny to go over the script and changes with Anya, and me to hang out and nose around

I intentionally avoided the area where Jenny was working. I didn't want to be seen as hovering. But when I went into one of the cabins looking for Ed Leighty, I walked in on one of the makeup ladies airbrushing Jen's nipples. Hers were that sexy shade of russet that redheads often sport, but they had to be dark to match Janine's. Of all the people in the place who had the least reason to gawk, I seemed to be the only one of the crew bustling around who did.

"Hey, Sam," she said. "What do you think?"

"They make you a dead match for Janine—oh, God, I don't believe I said that." My face flushed.

She and Judy, the makeup artist both giggled. No shortage of humor around here.

"That's Okay, Sam," she said. "It's all new to me too."

"We're just experimenting today," said Judy. "If you think she looks like DiBasil now, wait till we dye her hair."

"I can't wait," I said, and excused myself. I decided to get a beer out of my van and take a walk. I followed one of the hiking trails out of Tuscarora, and in three minutes I could see nothing but trees and hear nothing but birds and the faintest noise from the camp. Then I heard what sounded like a cry.

I rounded a bend in the trail and in a clearing I saw Marcie Graham face first against a tree, her sweat pants down around her knees, and one of the grips, a tall kid with greasy blond hair, was pushed up behind her. I was about to discretely slip away and go back the way I came when she cried out, "No, Ray! Stop it!"

"I was good enough for you before, Marcie. What's the matter with me now?"

"I don't want this. I told you, it's over."

He put an elbow in the small of her back and pinned her chest to the tree while his hands fumbled with the zipper on his jeans. "Oh, it'll be over, all right, bitch, in about five minutes."

I came up behind him and kicked him in the back of his left knee. The leg buckled, and I swung my right hand, beer can and all, and caught him on the side of his head. It wasn't the most elegant strike, but it worked. He fell sideways to the ground, rolled, and jumped to his feet. Maybe he was a stunt man in his spare time.

He reached for a sheath on his belt and pulled out a Buck Folding Hunter. He flipped it open and charged at me, totally irrational. I could see crystal meth in his wild eyes. I sidestepped his rush and tripped him, but he still caught my forearm on the way by. The blade was sharp, and I could feel the burn as it cut me. Ray sprawled headlong and before he could get up, I picked up a piece of wood the approximate dimensions of a baseball bat.

"Come on, Ray. Try it again. I'll bust your fucking head."

His eyes darted back and forth at us, and he crashed through the brush away from the clearing. "Are you…" I turned to Marcie and stopped in mid-sentence. She had picked up a rock the size of a baseball and was standing, pants still to her knees, ready to defend herself if I couldn't pull the freight.

I looked away. "Are you okay?"

She nodded, pulling up her sweats. "I think so. I feel like I should cry, but I'm too pissed off."

"Put yourself together. I'll take you back to camp. You can call the police. Or I will."

She looked at the blood seeping through my sleeve. "Oh, shit. He cut you, didn't he? Yeah, let's go."

We walked back to Tuscarora in silence. Marcie didn't want to talk, and I was busy thinking about frustrated men and sharp knives.

When we got back to the cabins, Ray had been there and gone, grabbing his duffel bag from his bunk and roaring off in his car with a spray of gravel. I let Marcie call the Sheriff's office. I called Kearny.

"I'm at Tuscarora. Got a live one for you, Mike," I said. "Name's Ray McCarthy. He just tried to rape one of the crew out here and he slashed me with a really sharp knife." I gave him the description of Ray and his beat-up 90s Oldsmobile. "If you're quick, you might catch him."

"How do you always end up in the middle of it all, Dunne?"

"Just lucky, I guess."

Jenny came running when she heard I'd been hurt. She started to cry when she saw the ugly slash across my forearm.

"Don't worry about me. I'll heal."

"You're going to need stitches." Ed said, wrapping the slash with gauze. "It's deeper than it looks."

"We'll pick up the tab for the ER," said Simon from behind me. He leaned in and said quietly, "Marcie told me what happened. Thanks for stepping in."

"I called the police already."

Simon frowned. "Well, I guess there was no getting around that, was there? McCarthy was a problem at times, but when he worked, he worked hard, and he knew what he was doing."

"Yeah, he looked like he knew he was doing meth," I said. "Anybody else in your crew I have to watch out for?"

Simon didn't answer. I was going to ask him if Ray had the hots for Janine, but decided I'd better let Kearny throw that pitch. "Let one of the guys drive you to the Hospital," Simon said.

"I'll take him," said Jenny, wiping her eyes.

"No, we need you here." He wrapped his fingers around her arm, and at that moment, I wanted to punch Simon in the teeth, contract be damned, but he led her away before action caught up with inspiration.

"Come on, Sam," Ed said. "I'll take you myself." We piled into Ed's Chevy Tahoe, and as we pulled out, I looked back to see Jenny, heading back to the cabins with Simon at one elbow and Anya at the other.

"It took some balls for you to go after Ray," Ed said. "He's a pretty tough guy. He's worked as a stuntman for a while. You can't do that if you aren't in shape and know how to fight."

"If I'd known that," I joked, "I might have thought twice."

Ed looked over at me and did a three-count before he spoke. "I don't believe that for a second, Sam. It just isn't your nature to let things go."

"Guilty as charged. Today, it was Marcie. If he got away with it, tomorrow it might be Jenny."

"Or Anya," said Ed, staring through the windshield.

"Are you two an item?"

He shook his head. "Not at all. I don't exist to her except as an extension of Simon's will. I think she's the real talent behind it all, but he gets all the credit as the brilliant director and producer. His movies are at least as much Anya's creations as his, but he pushes her behind him every time."

"Then why doesn't she go on her own?"

"You don't get it, do you? She worships Simon. And he treats her like he just scraped her off the heel of his Gucci loafer. She was crushed when he married Elizabeth. I thought maybe she'd give me a tumble then, but she hung on more determined than ever to please Simon."

"What about Janine? Where did she fit into the scheme of things?"

"Simon may be a genius at movie-making, but he was no genius with money. Last Light was faltering, and Elizabeth stepped in and put it all on a paying basis again. She hated Janine, but she saw her as a necessary evil to run the money-making machine." He shrugged. "No Janine, no Simon, no movies, no money."

"Why didn't they just get another woman for the lead?"

"She was Simon's pet. He'd never admit it, but she turned him on like no other woman alive. He'd never touch her, just look at her through the camera like some peephole voyeur. It's as if he has a collection of women around him, each one playing a unique role."

"I know women who behave that way: 'Queen Bees' we call them. A man for all occasions. One guy is the hard working provider, another one is the worshipper, one is the older mature friend, one is the sex toy. All in separate compartments. How do Simon's women feel about it?"

"They all accept it. That's how good a manipulator Simon can be."

"So everybody plays 'Simon says.'"

Ed nodded slowly. "That's about it."

And I just rode away and left Jenny with him.

XI

tall, lean Pakistani doctor named Makhi apologetically scrubbed the knife wound inside and out, which hurt like hell. He stitched it up; eleven stitches, two of them on the inside to pull the tissue together. He told me I was lucky that the blade cut longways and not across so it didn't cut any of my tendons. I agreed. I also considered myself lucky the blade caught my arm and not my neck. Makhi also said that the blade must have been scalpel sharp to cut so deeply and cleanly, even through my shirt.

Like the knife that cut Janine DiBasil's throat.

Ed waited for me outside. As we were heading for his truck, Kearny pulled in. He left the engine running and stood behind the open driver door. I guess I was supposed to take the hint, and when I didn't, he waved me over.

"Where's DeVon?"

"Back at the castle guarding the dungeon." He pointed at the bandage on my forearm. "You gonna press charges for that?"

I nodded. "Hell, yeah. Even if Marcie Graham doesn't have him arrested for assault and attempted rape, I can try for attempted murder and assault with a deadly weapon. You catch him, I'll testify."

"Too bad you weren't carrying. You could have saved the taxpayers a lot of money. He could have been notch number two on your tally."

It would have really been three, but I'd never tell anyone that, especially Kearny. "I figured you needed something to take your mind off the DiBasil case, so I let him bolt. I heard Hunter's bound over for the Grand Jury."

Kearny let out one of those snorting laughs of his that irritate the hell out of me. "Dick Hunter; what a name. Sounds like a gay porn star."

I didn't laugh. "Christ, Kearny, figure it out. It was an accident. There were three identical knives on the prop table. The kid picked up the wrong one."

I got Kearny's best ask-me-if-I-give-a-shit cop look, "We don't know that yet. Based on what I see, it's a fifty-fifty proposition. By the way, your buddy Ray McCarthy has an interesting jacket."

"That was quick."

"Thank VICAP; your tax dollars at work."

"You said interesting?"

"Three arrests for drunk and disorderly, four for simple assault, two for ag assault, and one for stalking, of all people, Jennifer Anniston."

"At least he has good taste."

"Keep your ears open, Sam. Something smells bad about this case." He didn't wait for a witty reply; he slid back onto the seat, put the car in gear, and closed the door as he drove away.

Two minutes later, I was in Ed's Tahoe heading back to Tuscarora. "So, did you ever have trouble with Ray before today?"

"No more than anybody else. He hired on when we filmed *Tree Walkers*. He was good with tools and never bitched when there was donkey work to be done."

"What about drugs?"

"Simon has a no-drug, no-booze policy for the set, but he's pretty much *laissez faire* as far as people on their own time go. If you show up and do your job, he doesn't push it."

"That seems risky to me. What if the cops raided the camp and found drugs? That could cause a cartload of problems for all of you."

"Doesn't seem to worry Simon at all."

"Was Ray a problem for any of the women? Other than Marcie, of course."

"Not that I know of. Just like the drug and booze issue, Simon doesn't seem to worry about who sleeps with who."

"Whom," I said on autopilot. Once a grammarian, always a grammarian.

"Whom sleeps with whom?"

"Forget I mentioned it, Ed. You said Ray is good with tools. How is he at sharpening them?"

"First rate. We needed the sharp copy of the knife for a scene when the blade comes through the tent and slits the canvas top to bottom in one fluid motion. Simon wanted it to be like a zipper pulling down. A dull knife would have jerked and torn things. You'll see the footage. It's one long slit down the side of the tent, perfectly smooth. It's horror film poetry."

I didn't push that line any further. That's why the City pays Kearny. "So, what's next?"

"We'll do some scenes with the other couple, Heather and Nick—Jacquie and Tyler in the script."

I leaned back in the seat and closed my eyes. "Wake me up when we get to Tuscarora." I really didn't want to sleep; I wanted to think, even though the thoughts were ugly as hell.

That night, the crew was filming outside one of the tents. Heather and Nick were snuggled in a double sleeping bag and Hunter, made up as the Lake Thing, was to climb through the slit in the side of the tent and stand over the sleeping couple, knife in hand.

I hadn't seen Dick since he was bailed out, but he seemed game enough, standing in full costume and makeup. It might have been charitable to give him a day or two to adjust, but I suppose Simon realized that he could be snatched away again any day and he wasn't taking chances. Simon wasn't on the set at the moment, so Anya got the couple arranged in the sleeping bag to his standard, Heather on her back so that her breast was exposed for the droolers in the audience, and Nick face down with an arm over her waist.

"Places." Anya called out. "Rolling," Shultz said.

"Action."

The camera panned across the sleeping couple and a dark shadow played over the side of the tent in the firelight, a man-shape with a long, wicked blade in its hand. Then nothing.

"What's the hold up?" Anya said. She turned to Smith. "Keep rolling." She walked around the tent where Dick stood motionless, staring down at the knife in his hand. "Come on, Dick. Go into the tent."

"I can't." Dick said, his voice muffled by the facial prosthetics. "I keep seeing Janine."

"Oh, Christ. Cut!" Anya stepped closer to Dick and wrapped her hand around the knife. She took it out of his hand by the blade. "Look, Dick. Watch." She put the edge against her throat and pulled it from one ear to the other. "See? It's okay," she said as if reassuring a frightened child. She dragged the blade across her palm. "Sharp as a tennis ball. You aren't going to hurt anybody, Dick. The real knife is gone." She was telling the truth. Kearny had it downtown in the evidence locker.

I saw Ed punch numbers into his cell phone and talk in a low voice. I didn't need to hear the conversation to know he was talking to Simon.

Anya's coaxing wasn't working. Dick stood, head down, a remorseful monster. It would have looked funny if I didn't know what it felt like to kill someone. When you've done that, whether or not it was deserved, it plays at the most inconvenient times on the back wall of your memory like a bad movie on a peep show loop.

Simon was there in minutes with Elizabeth in tow; full damage control mode. The unholy trio, including Anya, surrounded Dick and talked quietly while he stood and listened. I couldn't hear what persuasion Simon and his entourage used on him, but finally, Dick nodded his head and took the knife.

"Places!"

I thought of a little anonymous verse I'd seen once on a refrigerator magnet: "I'd give you my heart and let you just hold it; I'd give you my soul, but I already sold it." It seemed to fit all around.

That night, as we rode home from Tuscarora, I didn't have much to say. Jenny noticed. "What's the matter, Sam? Does it bother you that I'm doing topless stuff? I mean, it'll be my body but not my face on screen. It'll be like I was somebody else."

That's the whole point, I thought. You will be just like somebody else, and she's dead. "This whole thing bothers me, going ahead with the filming after Janine was killed. I could tell Dick didn't like it either. Based on the way Simon sweet talked him into doing the tent scene, he should be selling used cars or maybe running for president."

What I didn't say was that I was sure that somewhere in some digital archive, Simon would have Jenny captured forever, like a butterfly in a glass case and trot her out late at night to watch on his big screen TV. "You don't need me to tell you what to do, Jen."

"No, but I do value your input."

I grinned. "Isn't that what won you over in the first place? My input?"

Jenny laughed. "That helped, but it was your superior intellect that really snagged me."

"Eroticize intelligence."

"I'll vote for that."

"You can cast your ballot when we get home."

"Does this mean you want to caucus?"
"Not us, just you."

The eleven o'clock news spent a full five minutes on Hunter's preliminary hearing. Not exactly a media circus, it was more of a sideshow. The cameras weren't allowed inside the cramped magistrate's office, but they were waiting in the parking lot each one with a coifed news reader in front of it.

Sheriff Billings faced the cameras flanked by Kearny and Barry Henderson, the D.A. Since Billings was running for re-election that fall and the Henderson wasn't, Barry let Billings have the face time. "Today, Magistrate Harmon ruled that Richard Hunter is to be bound over for trial on a charge of manslaughter in the death of Janine DiBasil. Mister Hunter will be remanded to the County Jail. Bond has been set at one hundred thousand dollars. The County is grateful for the assistance of the Hanniston City Police Department's Homicide Division in this investigation. We can offer no further comment at this time, as the investigation is ongoing."

Simon and Elizabeth were conspicuously absent, but Charlotte Ledgerton, Scream's prototypical Yuppie lawyer, took her place at the microphones. She wore a doleful expression that made me expect a tear to filter through her perfect mascara, trickle down her cheek, and spot her flawless tweed suit. She was a better actor than most of Simon's cast. She read a terse prepared statement for the press:

"All of the cast and crew of *Lake Deadly* mourn the unfortunate death of Janine DiBasil in what is most certainly a tragic accident. We are convinced that Richard Hunter will be found innocent of any wrongdoing in this regrettable incident. Thank you."

When she stepped away from the microphones, the questions flew faast and furious. Especially whether the filming would continue. Charlotte shot a quick, "I can't comment at this time," and climbed into the passenger side of Ed's Tahoe.

The camera zoomed in on the deputies pushing Dick's head down and steering him into the back of the Sheriff's Crown Vic. He looked stricken, as if he still weren't sure what was happening. Over the shoulder of the local reporter, all big blonde hair and teeth, I saw Wendy Conn. It was as if she looked right out of the television screen at me, cold eyed and grim, then she smiled, but her eyes never changed.

XIII

The next day Jenny went to Tuscarora early and I stayed behind to work on music for the scenes Ed passed along. I was confident that I was doing a good job, but the possibility of Simon putting his hands on things set my teeth on edge.

I've always agreed with jazz man Benny Goldson, who said, "The better the script, the less music it needs."*Lake Deadly* needed more than average. Like so many low-budget films, money ruled and the cut corners often led to less than optimum results. I'm no filmmaker, but it seemed to me that rehearsing more and getting a scene right quickly was better than fumbling through the first six takes. Digital video encourages that behavior; you aren't paying for film and developing every shot. And after a half dozen takes, people get tired: actors, cameramen, sound techs, everybody, and it often results in a lackluster performance.

I could see it in my role as the deputy. What saved the scene was the fact that Janine was truly pissed off at Simon, and she channeled it into her role as being pissed off at me.

I worked the original riff I scored for the tree scene and made it a leitmotif, a recognizable peril theme that could be used throughout the movie. The point of view shot of the deputy approaching the tent would have seemed flat if it hadn't had the buildup of the theme.

I opted for minimal, following Goldson's doctrine, and played it on a nylon string guitar. Then I recorded a second track with the same notes played heavy-metal style with deep distortion. I put the tracks side by side and faded one into the other from the sweet clean nylon string tone to the ripsaw metal sound, ending abruptly when the tent flap opens.

The results were more than good. If Simon wasn't happy with that, tough shit. I wasn't changing a note.

Jen left me a plate of leftovers in the fridge; fettuccini Alfredo with shrimp and scallions. For someone who worked in a diner, she often surprised me with the quality and the diversity of her cooking. She said after slinging hash all day, she wanted something different, so she bought books and watched cooking shows and learned. I've often thought she should open her own restaurant, but her heart is set on being an English teacher, that is, if sudden stardom didn't change her mind.

I've always encouraged her to finish her degree and follow her dream, all the way to a Ph.D. if she wanted it, but as soon as she signed on to *Lake Deadly*, she cancelled her summer lit class to devote full time to the movie. I hoped it was a passing fancy.

It was Thursday evening and time for me to play my regular gig at Mike and Kelli's. I don't charge them nearly as much as I do other venues because they're my friends, and because I respect the blood and sweat that they pour into their business. Jenny didn't come with me this time; she was still at Tuscarora. The crew would start filming with her on Friday.

When I carried my amp and guitar into the bar, I saw Mike had made a change. Two years ago he hung a cardboard star over the corner where I play, and it's been there ever since. Tonight, there was a second star hanging beside it.

"What's up with the second star, Kelli?"

"Sam I am!" She seemed in better spirits tonight. "You're a two-star attraction now, music and the movies. We heard you landed a role in *Lake Deadly*."

"For all of fifteen seconds of face time," I said.

"But you'll get a screen credit. Four more, and you can put in for a SAG card," Mike said, coming around the bar. "Congratulations."

"Thanks." Then in a lower voice, "Any more word from Asswipe?"

Mike's smile faded. "No more visits, but every time a strange face comes in here, I break out in a cold sweat."

"Leave them to me. If they come any night, it'll be tonight when they know you regularly run music."

He nodded and turned back to the bar. I set up my gear and sat at the bar with a ginger ale waiting for the Lottery drawings to end. It used to be just the three-digit number, but now Pennsylvania runs Pick Two, Three, Four, and Five. I've never been too big on gambling myself; I have to scratch and scrape too hard for the money I have. There's more truth to "easy come, easy go" than most players want to admit.

After the Lottery crowd tore up their losing tickets, I sat on my stool and tuned my guitar. Most of the tables were full and so were half the stools at the bar. Over the last two years I'd built up a decent crowd of regulars for Mike and Kelli. I didn't want to see that come to an end.

As I was about to play my first song, a man and a woman strolled in. They weren't locals, and I smelled ASWI all over them. The woman was a

I sat on my stool and tuned my guitar.

dirty blonde in her mid-twenties, big hair and a little on the plump side. The guy was around my age, with hair going white; not grey, white in a modified ducktail the likes of which I hadn't seen since the mid-sixties. They took a table at the back of the room and each got a draft, which neither of them touched.

I started my set with "Clock Keep Tickin'," a bump and grind blues number with a slick instrumental intro. The crowd knew the song and received it well. I followed it with "Hourglass" and "I Can't be Bought." Everyone in the room was clapping and smiling, except the strangers at the table in the back corner.

"Here's another song that'll go on my next CD," I said. "It's brand new, and this is its first time in front of an audience" I trotted out "The Idea Song," Hedging against plagiarism and outright theft, I never played a song in public before I had a copyright filed, the laws being what they are, but ASWI had never heard of this one.

The audience ate it up. For the next hour, I played all originals that weren't ASWI-registered. When somebody yelled, "Play 'Blackbird,'" instead of "Play 'Free Bird,'" I smiled and shook my head. "My show's all originals," I said with a meaningful look at the strangers. I made a joke of it. "Songs you'll never hear anyplace else, and for a good reason." The crowd laughed. The agents didn't.

After two sets of original material, the strangers got up from their table, their beers still untouched. They passed my corner as they left, and as he passed, the white ducktail said with a Nashville twang in his voice, "You sound really good, but I didn't recognize any of your material."

Maybe he didn't recognize me either, face or name. "It's all my own stuff." I winked. "I hear Asswipe's on the prowl."

He gave me a laugh that curled his lip into a sneer. He didn't say, "Who?" He didn't say, "What?" Bullseye.

"See you around," he looked at my show card, "Sam Dunne."

When I ended my last set, Kelli had my Reuben and fries waiting at the bar. "I hope the crowd didn't mind my selections tonight."

She laughed. "They shouldn't. I went around before you started, and let them all in on the gag."

"Actually," Mike said, "People told me they liked it as well as when you play covers."

"I'm flattered," I said. "Let ASWI suck on that a while."

When I got home, Jenny was back from Tuscarora. I heard the shower running, so I slipped out of my clothes and pulled back the curtain to join her. She gasped, startled, and so did I. Her hair was coal black instead of red. I knew that was going to happen; what knocked me sideways was the sight of her pubic hair dyed the same color. I had a pretty good idea what that meant.

XIU

"You aren't coming out to Tuscarora, Sam?" Jenny stood framed in the bedroom doorway dressed in cutoff jeans and a T-shirt. I noticed right away she was braless, but I wasn't going to open that can of stink.

"Maybe later in the day. I'm going to stay here to work on the scenes Ed delivered yesterday. Sound track scores are a lot more work than I expected."

She came over to the breakfast nook and put her arms around my neck. "I don't know what time I'll be back, but not too late. Anya said we'll be doing all daylight work. The weather forecast says sunny all day."

I tilted my head into her chest, just to let her know her wardrobe status didn't slip past me. "If you get back early enough, we can go to Ernie's for wings. I'm sure you'll be too tired to cook."

"Sounds like a plan." She leaned in and pecked me on the cheek. "Get good stuff done."

In two seconds she was gone. I swirled the inch or so of coffee in my cup and berated myself for being a jerk, letting Jenny's nude performance bother me. If it were anyone but Simon, I told myself, it would be different. No, I decided, it wouldn't.

I watched the scenes Ed brought me. I watched them five or six times, and I just couldn't find anything compelling to hang a tune on. Maybe it was me, or maybe the scenes just weren't all that great. If Theodore Sturgeon was right, and ninety percent of everything is crap, I guess that applies to splatter films too.

Maybe the high-impact fright scenes were more inspiring than the filler stuff, like cars bouncing up a rutted country lane, smiling, laughing people passing a joint, or couples skinny-dipping in the lake and waving to a plane flying overhead. But it all needed music, and I had to deliver.

By lunch time, I furloughed my muse and decided to go to Tuscarora. Maybe the scenery would open a channel for me. The sun was warm in the pre-Memorial Day afternoon, and the sky was that shade of blue a camera never quite captures. I pulled in as the crew was finishing lunch.

Jenny was just walking into the wardrobe cabin with a pile of blouses over her arm. Seeing her at a distance with black hair gave me a start all over again, at least half because it made her look like I was seeing Janine's ghost.

I was foraging in the lunch leftovers when Ed came over. "How's the wrist?"

"It'll hurt my backhand at Wimbledon." I held up the wad of gauze and tape. "It looks a lot worse than it really is."

"The cops get a lead on Ray?"

"Not that I've heard, but he doesn't exactly confide in me."

Ed lowered his voice. "I think he might still be hiding out someplace close by."

"What makes you think so?"

"A couple of the crew think they've seen him at night skulking around."

"Why tell me? Tell Kearny and Wilson, or tell the Sheriff."

"Ever work in a carnival, Sam?"

"Can't say I have. You?"

"I traveled with Uncle Rainbow's Midway all over the southeast for two seasons. A hundred dollars a day cash and sleep in the trucks."

"A real dream job, huh?"

"It was when I was seventeen." Ed shook out a cigarette. "Carnies are a special brand of family, with an 'us and them' kind of loyalty when it comes to outsiders, especially the law. It's the same with this crew. You're show people; you understand. We look out for each other. Don't get me wrong, Sam. I don't like what Ray did to Marcie, and if I'd've walked in on it, I would have done the same thing you did, but we would have handled him ourselves, not called in the police."

"But he's a danger, Ed. And he'll be a threat to every woman in the camp if he's still here."

"And I have to worry about that too."

"And you're telling me this because you don't want to drop the dime, and you're hoping that I will." I was getting steamed and it was edging my voice.

Ed said nothing.

"And what that tells me is that as far as you're concerned, I'm not one of you."

Ed shook his head a little too fast. "No, no. Not at all. But you called 911 as soon as Janine was killed, and you called the cops when Ray cut you.

People expect that now. Ray still has friends in the crew. I have to work with these people day to day, Sam; you don't."

"I'm not a snitch. I know Kearny, but we aren't bosom buddies. If you're so edgy that Ray's still hanging around, tell Simon and let him call the cops. Or Elizabeth."

"I thought you might be worried that he'll try to get you for revenge." He paused. "Or Jenny."

Bringing Jenny into it was the last domino. "You know my back story, Ed?"

"Pretty much, yeah."

"Then you know why I'm not worried."

Ed nodded, dropped his cigarette on the ground and crushed it out with the toe of his boot. "I guess that's all there is to it." And he walked away.

I leaned against the picnic table and felt the butt of my Beretta poke into the small of my back. A small comfort, but a comfort nonetheless.

I decided I would give Kearny the tip about McCarthy, but not right away. My cell phone stayed in my hip pocket, because I knew that Ed would be watching for it. In the meantime, I'd be watching Jenny's back and mine.

The afternoon was taken up with shots of the principals gathering wood for the campfire and hiking through the trees. It was becoming obvious to me that the script was like a telephone line strung pole to pole, sagging between the high interest scenes, and the audience followed the line for the next hit of excitement, whether it be violence, shock, or sex.

A final scene for the day involved Heather and Nick playing in a grotto with a small waterfall. Ed had spotted this place before shooting started, and Simon had Willis write a scene around it. They splashed nude in the pool below the fall for a few takes, and Simon jerked his head to Anya. He said something to one of the grips, who took off at a trot back to the camp.

"Okay, Heather," said Anya. "Stand under the waterfall, back to the camera. Let's see how it looks." Heather climbed out of the pool and stood on the rock ledge where the water cascaded over her.

"Step forward a little." Anya looked at the camera's digital display. "Another inch or two." The result was a denser curtain of water, making Heather's body a little less distinct and blurring the tan line that made her look as if she were wearing a white thong. "Hold that position. Let's get a focus here." One of the grips held the bullseye just out of the falling water.

Anya shouted to be heard over the spattering drops. "Okay, Heather, when I call action, give me a three-count, raise your arms to ten-and-two, and turn to your right very slowly and move forward as you do, so you emerge from the water."

"Quiet on the set. Rolling."

"Action."

The result was one of the most sensuous things I'd ever seen; Anya evoked something atavistic that caught all of us, men and women by surprise. As Heather stepped forward, the water ran in rivulets down her body and as she stood on the ledge, the last droplets dripping from her nipples, it looked like the birth of a goddess. I suddenly understood what Ed was talking about. Anya was the creative brains of the outfit. She didn't need Simon; Simon needed her.

"Cut."

Simon said. "Smith, up on that overhang. Run the same thing again. Get the watcher point-of-view. Get both the kids in the shot." He turned to me. "Dunne, go up on the ledge with him. I want your head and shoulders in the shot." The grip he sent back to the camp handed me the deputy hat and shirt. "We'll see how you look as a Peeping Tom."

"You know that scene was originally written for Janine, don't you?" said Jenny. She startled me. I didn't hear her come up behind me while I was changing my shirt. "Anya said it would be too tough to CGI with the water, so they gave it to Heather instead."

I put an arm around her shoulder. "I'm just as glad they did. You'd look incredible in that shot, but with your own face, not somebody else's."

I crouched on the rock above the grotto and Smith hunkered down behind me. "Let's see it," Anya called up to Smith. Below, she and Simon studied a small wireless video monitor. "Pull back from the waterfall until the deputy's head and shoulder are in frame."

"Try it once. Sam," Simon said. "Take off the hat and put it beside you to your left." He looked into the monitor and gave a thumbs-up.

"Places." Heather stepped back into the waterfall. "Action."

My part was easy. All I had to do was lie on the rock and enjoy the view. Two tries from overhead, and Simon and Anya were satisfied. Heather, teeth chattering, pulled on her sweats and toweled her hair. "Good job, Heather," said Anya. You'll like how you look."

Back at the camp, Ed had pizza delivered for dinner. "I'm surprised everybody here doesn't weigh three hundred pounds," I said, putting a flopping slice with pepperoni onto a paper plate. "This isn't exactly the Paleo Diet."

Jenny laughed. "You just can't eat a lot of anything. Too many carbs and too much fat in most of the food they feed us. Give me a plate of Dora's steak and eggs any day."

"Has Ed said anything to you the last day or so?"

"Besides 'hello,' not really. Why?"

"I had an odd conversation with him this afternoon. He thinks Ray McCarthy may still be hiding out in the woods near here. I told him to call the police and let them know. He wanted me to do it."

"And you said no."

"I said no."

"Maybe Simon wants you to do it but won't ask you himself. That sounds like his brand of management."

"Or maybe Simon doesn't want Ed to do it, and Ed's afraid for his job. Point is, Jen, don't wander off by yourself, especially at night."

Jenny's eyes got wide and she said, "Ch-ch-ch-ch-ch-ch. Hah-hah-hah-hah-hah-hah."

"That's the worst imitation of *Friday the 13th* I ever heard." Jerry, the FX guy sat on the bench next to me, laughing. Marcie and a couple of the other crew members joined us. I caught Jenny's eye and gave a short shake of my head. She got the message.

"This whole place reminds me of Camp Crystal Lake with a fresher coat of paint," I said.

"Naah," said one of the grips, a scrawny kid known to the others by the unfortunately fitting nickname Fetus. "Maybe Camp Gucci Lake with all those tennis courts for young yuppie spawn."

"So, how do you guys feel about going ahead with the movie?"

"It's our jobs, man. I mean, Janine was a classy lady, and she wasn't stuck up or anything. She didn't treat us like peons, but if the wheels stop turning, we're out here in flyover country with no ticket home."

"Yeah," said Jerry. "If an ironworker falls twenty stories off a building, they take off their hard hats, say a few words, and get back on the horse. Shit happens."

I was a little surprised at their callous attitude, but I reminded myself that these guys were part of the generation that grew up watching the kind of movie they were making and playing *Grand Theft Auto* and *Call of Duty*.

For them death was mundane and no big deal. Just hit the reset button. But there was no reset for Janine.

Jenny stood up. "I have to go over to makeup now. We're shooting a twilight scene by the lake tonight."

"I'll walk you over," I said. I nodded to the crew. "See you guys later." When we were out of earshot, I said, "Damn, those guys are cold."

"Well, if one of them got electrocuted holding a wire in the lake, do you think Janine DiBasil would refuse to go on? It's like Simon said, they're making money."

She had me there, so I just shut up.

The evening was perfect. Anya had Smith set up the camera to silhouette Jenny and Bobby against a sunset that reflected half of the dying sun in the still water and faded from rose to violet into night.

"Rolling."

"Action."

Bobby picked up a guitar and fumbled through a few chords. Jenny put a joint in her mouth (really tobacco twisted up in Zig-Zag papers) and lit it. She took a long drag and leaned forward, putting her mouth over Bobby's. When their lips parted, wisps of smoke danced around their heads. They laughed, and Bobby set down the guitar. He turned and took Jenny's face in his hands and kissed her tenderly.

"Zoom it." Anya hissed, and the camera's eye shot across the lake where a dark shape barely broke the surface, and concentric ripples radiated like rings of evil. Behind her, Marty stood with a control pad operating the one bladed propeller from an RC boat tied to a fishing sinker.

"Keep rolling. One more time. Same action as soon as the ripples die down. Action."

Jenny and Bobby ran the scene again. "Cut. Same action from the front this time. Let's move before we lose the light."

Smith moved the camera to shoot them head on. "Rolling."

"Action."

Jenny and Bobby went through the motions again, playing the guitar, lighting the joint, kissing, but this time, instead of saying, "zoom it," Anya said, "Reaction."

Jenny broke away from the kiss, her head swiveling away from Bobby toward the middle of the lake, her eyes suddenly wide. "What was that?"

"What?"

"Out there on the lake. I thought I heard something."

"Probably a trout snapping at dinner."

Jenny looked across the water. "Yeah, you're probably right." She looked back one last time with anything in her face but reassurance.

"Cut. One more time while we have the light."

"Jenny, look harder at the lake the first time. Furrow your brow." It was Simon this time. "Make us see your instinct kicking in."

"Rolling."

"Action."

When they finished the scene, Anya said, "Wrap it. We lost the light."

Marty was reeling in his gadget with a fishing pole. "That's a nifty little item," I said as he shook the water from it.

"It works. One thing you learn making low-budget films: the best special effects cost less than five dollars." When I made a quizzical face, he said, "Fritz Lang filmed the robot scene in *Metropolis* with a hand cranked camera and a couple of lights. Small budgets and low tech make you use big imagination and hard work to put what you want on screen. Anybody with a half a mil can CGI anything, but for my money, it comes out looking like somebody playing a video game."

"Yeah, I know what you mean. I've seen plenty of those on the SyFy channel. We have a similar idea in music: let the guitar do the talking; don't bury it under a dozen effects."

"Amen, brother."

Back at the camp, someone had built a fire in the campfire circle, a ring of benches around a rough stone fire pit, and as people put away their gear, in ones and twos, they drifted out to the fire, like a tribe of primitives to stay in the safety of the light. I decided instead of heading home right away, I'd stay for a while to see what I could pick up from the general conversation.

Pretty soon, a bottle of wine started circulating, and then another. A half-dozen conversations sprang up around the circle, most of them about whoever wasn't there at the moment. They were all laughing, joking with each other and looking away from the real horror on the set. Maybe I was the one with the wrong attitude.

Marcie sat down beside us. "You did good today," she told Jenny. "Janine couldn't have done any better."

"Thanks, but Anya gets most of the credit. She worked me pretty hard the last two days to get me into the part."

Marcie laughed. "I believe that. She knows what Simon wants."

Across the fire, I saw Simon leaning against a tree outside the circle. He was staring at Jenny. More than staring, his eyes were crawling all over her. He must have felt me looking at him, because he looked my way and met my gaze. Instead of blinking, or looking away, his eyes locked on mine and he smiled. Someone threw a log on the fire and the flames flared for a second, and when they receded, Simon was gone.

I stood up and took Jenny by the elbow. "Let's go, Jen. I'll follow you back to town."

She was about to protest, but the look on my face must have persuaded her otherwise.

"What's the matter?"

"We'll talk about it when we get home."

But we didn't, really. I told Jenny I thought Simon was making her a replacement for Janine in his off screen fantasies, not just in front of the camera. She said I was making a lot out of nothing. I said it worried me. She said the first time he said or did anything out of line, she'd let me know and I had her permission to kick his ass. In the meantime, don't rock the boat.

I respected Jenny's judgment, but I didn't like it.

XV

I decided the next day to put a little distance between myself and the set. Maybe Jenny was right. Maybe I was reading too much into Simon's behavior. He was weird, but so were most of the other people in the cast and crew. I didn't want to kill Jenny's chances by picking a fight, so I figured staying away was the best policy.

That didn't make it any easier for me to focus on work. Ed had given me two more scenes to score, both of them with Nick and Heather. They were both pretty good; in fact I thought Heather was as good as Janine and could have done her role as well, of course she also could have died as horribly if she were Simon's goddess.

The day was a slow one for me. Everything I wrote seemed to sound like everything I'd done before, not pursuit of a leitmotif, but repetition, pure and simple. I was frustrated and ready to start throwing things.

When the phone rang, the interruption was almost a blessing. At least it was till I saw the caller I.D. It was Kearny.

"Dunne. Can you come out to Tuscarora?"

"Well, I'm in the middle of something right now."

"I'll rephrase that. Come out to Tuscarora. Now. We found Ray McCarthy. He's dead."

"How—?" The line was dead too. Kearny had already hung up.

By the time I pulled into the parking area at Tuscarora, six cop cars and an ambulance were all pulled in at haphazard angles, their roof racks flashing like a seventies disco. The cast and crew were standing outside the dining hall hemmed in by a gang of deputies. Kearny was standing off to the side talking with Ed Leighty and Sheriff Billings.

When Kearny saw me, he broke away from the conversation. "So, Dunne, we got another cold one."

"What happened?"

"That's what I'm trying to figure out. A couple of the crew were lugging camera equipment out into the woods and they found McCarthy's Olds Ciera parked on an overgrown access road. They walked up to it and saw Ray in the front seat, slumped like he was asleep. Then they got closer and heard the flies."

"Flies?"

"Oh, I forgot, you're not a trained homicide detective. Flies tend to gather around a corpse, especially if he's had a few hours in warm weather to ripen him up a little."

"So how did he die?"

"You can't guess?" Kearny raised an eyebrow. "His throat was cut from ear to ear, just like Janine DiBasil's."

Before I could respond, I saw Simon and Elizabeth come around the corner of the dining hall with Wendy Conn. "So, Kearny, you invited the press to the picnic too?"

He looked over his shoulder. "You mean Wendy? Naah, she was here when they found McCarthy's body. She was interviewing Schiff about the movie and DiBasil's death."

I ground my teeth. Simon would do anything to get more publicity for himself and his film, including pad a hit piece on me for *Nightside*. "She talk to you yet?"

Kearny shook his head. "Nope. When she tried to pry details of the DiBasil investigation out of me, I gave her the D.A.'s number. I'm out of it, or I was once the charge was dropped to manslaughter, but now it looks like DeVon and I are back in the yoke."

"You think the two are related?"

"What do you think? Two stiffs in a week, both working the same job, killed the same way? Coincidence?"

"Sounds like you've got it all under control. Why do you need me out here?"

"Let's take a walk," Kearny said, and we headed toward the woods. Jenny saw me about the same time I saw her in the crowd by the dining hall. I waved and pointed to Kearny. I shrugged, and she gave Kearny the finger. That's my girl.

A mile out of camp, I heard voices, then we rounded a bend in the trail and I saw the yellow police line tape. Three deputies and DeVon stood beside Ray's blue rust bucket Olds while a crime scene tech took pictures. A little bald man with thick glasses was leaning into the car through the open passenger window. I recognized him from years of the TV news as Rudolph Hech, the Coroner.

"So why do you need me out here, Mike? You have a whole team, it looks like."

"You'll see." He came up behind the photographer. "Step back, Donna. Okay, Dunne. Tell me, is that the knife McCarthy used to slash your arm?"

I looked through the open door of the Olds and almost retched. McCarthy was slumped behind the wheel, the entire front of his T shirt black with dried blood all the way to his lap.

Kearny had done this to me once before, surprising me with the corpse of a dead friend in the morgue to see my reaction. I threw up that time, and then I knocked him on his ass. This time I wouldn't give him the satisfaction. It took me a minute to locate the knife. It was lying loosely in his right hand. It was a Buck Folding Hunter. If it wasn't the same knife, it was its twin.

I took two deep breaths to clear my head before I said anything. "Looks like it, but if you've seen one Buck Knife . . ."

"So, I shouldn't be surprised if your blood turns up on the blade, right, Sam?"

I ignored the jibe. "Since Ray's had time to draw flies, what time does Doctor Death say he died?"

Hech looked over the roof of the car at me and said in a flat, matter of fact voice, "Between nine thirty-seven and nine forty-seven last night."

I blinked. "How do you know down to the minute?"

Hech grinned. "The marvels of forensic science." He pointed to McCarthy's lap. "All that blood soaked into his jeans." Hech held up a plastic evidence bag with a sliver pocket watch. "It gummed up his watch, which stopped at nine forty-seven. Allowing a ten minute margin for the blood to coagulate and..."

"Okay, I get it."

"Besides, temperature, decomposition, rigor mortis and other factors all agree with the nine forty-seven ballpark."

"Last night was Thursday, Kearny. Guess where I was."

"Mike and Kelli's?"

"You got it. After that, I was with Jenny all night. Ask her."

"I probably will. Nothing personal, Sam, but in the motive department, you and the Graham girl are the top two candidates so far."

"I suppose McCarthy wasn't the remorseful type who'd cut his own throat."

"I don't know about his personality type," said Hech, "but from what I see, this is no suicide. The angle of the cut and the depth from one end to the other indicate somebody cut him from outside the car through the open window, right to left."

"You said you hit McCarthy, right, Sam?" Kearny said, slouching against the fender of the Olds.

"I clocked him on the side of his head with a beer can in my hand."

Hech nodded. "That's consistent with the cut on the right side of his face."

"How many times?"

"Just one."

Hech walked around to the open driver door and reached in. "We found this." He pulled a shock of Ray's hair away from his face. When he did, Ray's head tilted back and I saw the raw meat of his slashed throat. "There." Hech pointed to a mark the size of a fifty-cent piece just above Ray's left eyebrow. "It looks like somebody sapped him. He bled out before it had enough time to swell or bruise noticeably."

Kearny said, "So whoever did this caught McCarthy off guard, knocked him out with some blunt instrument, then used the guy's own knife to cut his throat."

"Which means?"

"Which means it could have been someone McCarthy knew, or some stranger who crept up on him. Maybe he was asleep."

Hech pointed to blood stains on the seat and floor mat. "It doesn't look as if the killer moved him. The amount of blood all over the driver's area and the steering wheel is consistent with the usual 10 pints or so per capita. We'll test it, of course, to make sure it's all his, but at the moment, I'm guessing nobody else contributed to the puddle." He opened a syringe kit and pulled out a wicked long spike.

"You think he has enough blood left for you to draw any?" I said, trying to look nonchalant.

"Don't want his blood," Hech said, prying Ray's left eye open with a gloved thumb and forefinger.

Before I could look away, he deftly plunged the needle into Ray's eyeball and filled the syringe. "Vitreous fluid; wonderful for drug and alcohol scans and general chemical analysis. Did you know that the fluid in the eyeball can even be analyzed after embalming? It's relatively isolated from the other bodily fluids and is relatively unaffected by things like redistribution and hemoconcentration."

"Doc knows his shit," said Devon, chuckling.

"By the way, Sam, we put a hustle on the prints on the knife that killed Janine DiBasil. Guess whose were on it."

"Ray's?"

"And about half the cast and crew."

"No surprise there. This is one of those operations where everybody does every job as needed. Lots of people probably handled the knife."

"Your prints were conspicuously absent."

"Oh good. I guess I can sleep tonight."

DeVon looked over toward Ray's corpse then gave me his two-foot smile. "Pleasant dreams."

Kearny stayed behind at the crime scene, and I found my own way back to the camp with an admonition from him to keep my mouth shut. I caught myself thinking, where was Hunter when this went down, and that Kearny probably already knew.

Back at the camp, the Sheriff was interviewing everyone from the cast and crew, one at a time, in the dining hall. Jenny was standing outside.

"They talk to you yet?" I asked.

"Yeah, but we aren't allowed to leave. What did Kearny want?"

"I'll tell you later. What's going on over there?"

Ed, Shultz, and Smith, the cameraman, were setting up a tripod. One of the grips came out with the camera case. In a minute, the camera was on the stand and Smith had his eye to the viewfinder. I walked over and asked Ed, "What are you guys doing?"

The grip stood beside the ambulance with the White Balance card. "We're getting some footage of the cop cars. Never know when we might be able to use it."

Anya's words rang in the back of my head: "There'll always be another horror film."

"Besides, if I wanted to set up a shot like this, I'd have to donate five hundred bucks to the Police Athletic League." I turned and Simon and Elizabeth were standing behind me.

"So who's Wendy Conn talking to now?"

"She's gone," said Elizabeth. "In one way, it was lucky she was here when Ray's body was discovered. She'll file the story with the wire service, and we won't be besieged by reporters. Opportunity is where you make it."

"I suppose you had a long chat with Wendy about me."

"Don't flatter yourself, Dunne," Simon said. "Your name came up in the general discussion, but she was more interested in Janine's accident than anything else."

I'll bet. Maybe Simon didn't know she was writing about the "Sam Dunne Jinx," but I wasn't giving him the benefit of the doubt. I was convinced that he'd sell his own mother to promote a film.

In a few minutes, Kearny was back at the camp. He and Hech spoke with the paramedics and they climbed into the ambulance. They pulled out of the parking lot and drove around to the access road to pick up Ray's body.

When Kearny was done talking to the Sheriff, I caught up with him and Devon on their way to car. "Jenny's already given her statement. Is it okay if we go now?"

"Sure. Go ahead; You'll be around if I need to talk to either one of you, right?"

"Is this your subtle way of saying, 'don't leave town?' Actually, I'll be away for a few days; playing in Myrtle Beach."

"Oh yeah? Well, do me a favor and stay in touch."

"I'll only be as far away as your phone."

"Speaking of which," Kearny said. "Look what I found." He held up an evidence bag with a cell phone in it. The screen was spidered with cracks and there was dried blood crusted on its case.

"McCarthy's?" I said.

"Seems so," Devon said. "It was under his body. We found it when the meat wagon took him."

Kearny held the bag by a corner, studying the phone. "Once it's been dusted for prints, We'll find out who he was talking to."

"Why wait?" said Devon. He took the bag from Kearny and carefully cradled the phone in his palm. He held in the power button and the screen lit up. He drew a finger across the screen, lightly at first, then with a little more pressure. "Look at that. The man didn't lock his phone."

Devon tapped at the screen. "Recent calls. Here's one from last night, around eight o'clock. Looks like fourteen minutes. Whattaya think, Mike? Should I?"

"Oh yeah."

Devon tapped the icon and McCarthy's cell phone connected. He tapped the loudspeaker icon and we heard it ring. Three times. Four times. "This is Anya Savage. I can't talk right now. Please leave me a message."

"Excuse us," said Kearny. He and Devon walked away toward the office cabin where Anya and Ed were talking with Billings and Hech. As Kearny passed a deputy, he said something to him and pointed to us. The deputy nodded, and I took that as permission to leave.

"Aren't we going?" Jenny said.

"In a minute. I want to see what happens next."

Kearny and Wilson walked up behind Anya and Kearny said something to her I couldn't hear. Anyone who lives in Pennsylvania, where one in seventy-one drivers hits a deer on the road every year, can appreciate the phrase "deer in the headlights look." It was all over Anya's face.

Kearny, Billings, and Wilson took Anya into the dining hall, leaving Ed staring after them. I wondered if Simon still had the camera running.

"I wish I could hear that conversation," I said.

"Me too."

"We'll find out what's up soon enough. Let's get out of here."

Neither of us was really hungry, but we went to Ernie's anyway, if for nothing more than a different atmosphere. Ernie's is noisy and smoky — from ribs and wings cooking, not cigarettes — and everybody there behaves, as F. Scott Fitzgerald wrote in *The Great Gatsby*, "according to the rules of an amusement park."

I've never been as big on wings as Jenny, which is funny because she's the health food nut and the gourmet cook. I guess we all have a secret vice or two. But tonight, even Ernie's wings didn't turn her into a ravaging carnivore. I have to admit that the sight of Ray McCarthy grinning from two mouths didn't do much for my appetite, either.

"So," I said, "Any word about whether Simon will keep shooting?"

"I didn't hear anything one way or the other. Anya told me to be out at eight o'clock tomorrow, so I guess they plan to go on."

I shook my head. "I know losing somebody like Ray isn't like losing the star, but Christ, I'd at least take a day or two off to regroup."

"You aren't Simon," she said and reached across the table to take my hand. "And I'm glad."

"I'll take that as a compliment. Finish your beer. It's time to go home."

XVI

The next day, Jenny was out the door early and I malingered at the breakfast table. Gordon Lightfoot once sang, "I'm on my second cup of coffee and I still can't face the day." A shot of Yukon Jack in it helped a lot. I felt an eerie sense of *deja vu* at being a homicide suspect again. I had an airtight alibi, but it was still unnerving to be under Kearny's microscope.

At forty-seven, I've reached the point at which I think about the future less in terms of potential successes and more in terms of spin control; when the hammer of old age comes down on me, how to soften the blow.

I looked across the living room to the two opposing walls that symbolized my bifurcated life. On one wall hung guitars and other stringed instruments, against the other stood bookshelves that reached nearly to the ceiling, crammed with the best in English and American literature. Between my music career and my Master's degree in English, I've managed to live well enough, I suppose, although there are times when I think I might have done better concentrating on just one thing.

Any time people ask me which is my real job, rock star or English prof, I say, "Depends on what time of day it is." My grandfather used to tell me, "Don't ride two horses with one ass, you'll end up falling between them and get trampled." There's wisdom in that, but so far I've managed to stay on top of it, and it's a little late in the game to start second guessing myself now.

Any time things trouble me, the guitar always turns me around. One of my old girlfriends once told me that watching me play my first set was like watching a fist slowly uncoil. It was that solace that I went after now.

I took my Martin off the wall and started my tuning ritual. The electronic tuner is one of the greatest gifts technology ever gave the guitarist, making it easy to plug in and tune accurately on a stage full of people all doing the same thing, but when I'm by myself, I prefer tuning by ear. It's not just the sound, but the feel of strings coming into tune that makes me feel the instrument and I are extensions of each other.

I started with the low E string and worked up. Most people I know start with the high E string and work down, but since the thicker strings create more tension on the neck to affect the others; I've found that if they're settled first, the thinner strings won't pull them out of tune, as the reverse may do for the thin ones. It's unconventional, but it works for me.

Once the guitar was in tune, I ran a few old blues tunes, a couple of folky finger picking riffs, and even a classical piece by Fernando Sor. By the time that was over, I felt ready to take another run at the scenes that stalled me yesterday. I started with the love scene in the tent. The shots from various camera angles were edited into a series of fade-in overlays that looked cheap and tacky yesterday but today looked less tawdry and more sensuous.

I laid down a slow arpeggiation with breathy add-nine chords, accenting every third note to skew the rhythm. I put that on a loop and reached for my old Gibson Les Paul. I developed a lazy, almost insouciant single note riff to counterpoint the acoustic background, then I put both in the computer. I copied the melody line into six separate tracks and applied a different effect to each. Mixing three of them, I got an almost ethereal sound grounded by the acoustic fingerpicking.

No bass sound seemed to fit, including a deep synthesized string patch from my Roland keyboard, so I finally opted for low string chords played with light distortion and a lot of sustain. By the time I was done, I had something even Simon should appreciate. I couldn't wait to play it for Jenny. Move over, Santana.

I was burning the finished product onto a DVD when someone knocked at the door. I looked through the peephole and recognized Ed's nose. "Come in, man," I said. "What's up?"

He hesitated for a few seconds then stepped inside, closing the door behind him. He looked around the room almost as if to reassure himself that we were alone, then he said, "Did you hear what's going on?"

"I guess not, or you wouldn't be here to tell me."

"Yesterday, before we called the cops, Simon had the crew shoot footage of Ray dead in the car."

"For what?"

"He and Elizabeth told Anya that if the picture gets scrapped, he'll make a documentary for one of the true crime cable channels."

"And Anya told you." He nodded. "So, Ed, who else knows?"

"Maybe nobody, maybe everybody. No one's talking about it."

Suddenly, filming the cop cars in the parking lot made more sense to me. Like Elizabeth said, opportunity is where you make it."Can he get away with it without a whole new set of contracts?"

"The boilerplate clause in everybody's Lake Deadly contract about making 'filming of' documentaries probably covers it if everybody grabs a corner and pulls to stretch it. I'm guessing the barracuda okayed it."

You mean Charlotte Ledgerton?"

"Yeah. And, Sam, they set up a video cam in the dining hall while the interviews were going on. Simon offered it as a 'courtesy' to the cops, but he had a wireless feed from the camera going to a recorder, He's got a copy of it all."

"Does Sheriff Billings know about this?"

"I don't think so. Probably not. I'm guessing it's not illegal, since the camera was running with the cops' approval and no one was videoed without their knowledge."

I wondered whether the idea was Simon's or Elizabeth's. It didn't matter. Either one of them was slippery enough to concoct the scheme. They probably ran it past Charlotte Ledgerton in some emergency meeting to see how it would fly legally. "Is Anya on board with this?"

Ed grabbed a handful of the hair on the back of his head and twisted it through his fingers, something I noticed that he did when he was agitated or nervous. "Yeah. It would mean her job if she said no."

"And yours."

He nodded. "Besides, if Simon said, 'chop off your foot,' she'd ask him, 'which one, or both.'"

"Simon says. The next question is why are you telling me this, Ed?"

The words tumbled out. "Because you are the one person who stands up to Simon. The rest of us have to wait on his good pleasure. This is just wrong, but none of us can do a damned thing about it. Maybe you can't either. I guess I just needed to talk with somebody about it."

"And while we're on the subject of Anya, what was that business with her cell phone?"

"Anya and I were in the office most of the evening — till almost midnight. I was there when Ray called her. He wanted paid for the time he worked. Anya told him she couldn't do anything about it."

"For twenty minutes?"

"They argued about it, but that's as far as it went."

"Why'd he call Anya? Why not you? Or Elizabeth if he wanted his money?"

"I guess he thought Anya was an easier touch for it. They always got along."

"Is Kearny buying this?"

"He said he's keeping an 'open mind,' whatever that means."

I knew from experience exactly what that meant. It meant don't leave town. "Ed, it's a little early in the day, but do you want a beer?"

"Does Sheriff Billings know about this?"

He shook his head. "If I have one, I won't stop till I pass out. I'd better just go."

When the door closed behind him, I went for that beer myself. Ed just set me on the edge of a tall razor blade, and whichever way I fell off, I was going to land in a pile of broken glass.

XVII

That night Joe had me booked at the Crescent Inn in Dunningstown, about fifty miles away. Jenny came home tired from the set.

"I can't believe it," she said. "It's harder work than the diner."

"They probably have to work you twice as hard because it's all new to you. They're training you as they go."

"I guess," she said, "but if you don't mind, I'm staying in tonight and going to bed early."

I can't say that I blamed her, really. Sitting watching me for three hours while I do the same material she's heard plenty of times loses its luster after a while. That coupled with the barflies hitting on her all night made staying home an attractive option.

I keep my gear in the back of my minivan most of the time to save wear and tear on the equipment and on me loading it in and out, so I didn't have much to carry to the elevator, just my guitar and my Samsung tablet. The tablet had files of music and lyrics for all the material I did, my own and others'.

I used to carry a notebook that sat on the small attached music stand next to my microphone, but turning the pages to find a specific song takes a lot longer than tapping the screen. Progress. An added bonus: if someone requests a song and I don't have the words, I can download the lyrics in less than a minute and keep the crowd happy.

I got to the Crescent about seven, an hour before I had to play and found the lot about half full. The supper crowd was dwindling, and the drinking crowd would be rolling in from eight o'clock on. The shadow-box stage at the Crescent is mid-sized, which means it's too small for a full-sized band but just big enough that a solo player looks lost on it. I've learned to set up my rig in a tight cluster, including the spot lights and leave the rest of the stage dark. That way the stage doesn't swallow me up.

The restaurant is big enough for me to use a p.a. system instead of a self-contained amp, and the house takes a line from my p.a. head to feed through the whole restaurant. I don't know whether people at the urinals appreciate it, but it's comprehensive.

I was taking the last of my equipment out of the van when I saw a blue Chevy van with Tennessee plates pull into the lot. The driver door opened and I saw the white ducktail climb out. In a minute, the stout woman joined him and they strolled toward the front door. Once I got inside, I called Duane Parks, the manager, over.

Duane is a little guy with heavy-framed glasses and a diamond stud in one ear, and he is in top shape and a nasty street fighter. When some drunk starts raising hell in the Crescent, he doesn't always call the bouncers, "send in the clowns," as he puts it. I've seen him put guys twice his size on the floor and drag them out face down by their ankles to the parking lot. Duane always dresses in black, and if you look closely, you'll see the wear patterns in his shirts at the small of his back where he keeps a .32 automatic in the waistband of his slacks.

"See the couple waiting for a table? The tall guy with the white hair? He and the woman are ASWI agents." What I didn't tell him was that I suspected they were there because of me.

"Ooh, I'm so scared." He clutched his shoulders and faked a shiver. "You don't think he'll hit a guy with glasses, do you?"

I told him how I handled my show for Mike and Kelli, but he shook his head. "Just do your regular playlist, and we'll see what he says. Then he'll see what Danny says."

"You're the boss."

"No, Danny's the boss."

Danny Vecchio, the owner of the Crescent was the forty-something son of Anthony "Little Tony" Vecchio, local mob boss and numbers kingpin for Central Pennsylvania. The Feds have always suspected that Danny laundered money for his dad, but so far they haven't proved it. If the ASWI reps thought they were going to lean on Danny Vecchio, that could be interesting.

Most of the time, unless I'm doing a concert appearance, I just walk out, sit on my stool, and start playing. No fanfare, no big buildup. That's okay with me. I know I'm no superstar and I don't expect superstar treatment. Since *Requiem* came and went, I'm playing some bigger and better venues, and being better paid, but for the most part, I'm still what I was before, a barroom balladeer and unapologetic about it.

As I tuned up, I saw Whitey and Big Hair take a table in a back corner where they wouldn't be too prominent. I smiled and waved to them, but they pretended not to notice.

I opened my set with "Searchin' for a Vein," the lead track from *Requiem*, and let the music take over. Bar and club work, especially for a solo performer, is a high-wire act with no net. It's all you; succeed on your own, or fall on your own with nobody to catch you.

The crowd, many of them regulars, took the song well and gave me the applause that set the tone for the rest of the evening. I couldn't see what Whitey and Big Hair were doing, but I had a feeling it wasn't drinking the drafts they ordered.

I followed "Searchin' for a Vein" with my acoustic version of Dire Straits' "Sultans of Swing" and Bob Seger's "Turn the Page," the road warrior's anthem. The crowd was getting into it. Halfway through J. J. Cale's "Money Talks," a commotion erupted in the back corner. I followed standard operating procedure when you're working a club and trouble starts: keep playing and play loud. If things go right, management sorts it all out before the crowd notices and everybody else gets into the act.

The upshot was that Whitey and his girlfriend left, escorted by four of Duane's people in the middle of my next song. On the way out, Whitey shot me a look that would derail a freight train and pointed a finger gun at me. I smiled back. Duane told me later how it all went down.

"I watched your friends for a few minutes, and they were both punching their cell phones like crazy while you were playing. Maybe they were typing in your song list. I really don't like their brand of shit, so I had Doris go by with a pitcher of beer. Seems she stumbled and dumped the whole thing on the table, their phones, and their laps.

"The ducktailed guy jumped up and started mouthing off at her, and I happened to be in the vicinity, so I said to him, 'I'm the manager. Is there a problem, sir?' He said, 'That bitch dumped beer all over us and our cell phones.' I said, 'I'll have you know that 'that bitch' is my little sister. I'm going to have to ask you to leave.' I gave him a three count while the boys formed up behind me and then said, 'While you can,' and stuffed two hundred dollar bills in his shirt pocket. 'No hard feelings.'"

I imagined Whitey's face when he looked over Duane's shoulder and saw four t-shirted bouncers with arms bigger than his thighs standing behind him. I'd leave too.

The rest of the night was uneventful, a good gig by most people's estimation, but I knew that from this point onward, the gauntlet was down; Whitey was making it personal.

XVIII

spent the better part of Sunday packing for Myrtle Beach. I wished Jenny could come along; it was a twelve-hour drive and her company would have made it more pleasant. Of course what bothered me the most was leaving her behind to work on the movie. I thought the atmosphere around the *Lake Deadly* set was toxic, and I hated to think any of that venom would rub off on her.

I hadn't been out to Tuscarora since my command appearance for Kearny. I just didn't want to be around Simon and Elizabeth, and that whole scene. Besides, I wanted as little of my face in that documentary as possible. By the way, Jen liked my love-scene motif. She said it wasn't "Europa," but it came in a close second. Maybe if I added a flute . . .

I relented and rode out to the camp late in the afternoon and got there as people were carting gear back from a location shoot by the lake. Jenny saw me and ran over, throwing her arms around me and giving me a deep kiss.

"Hold that pose."

We looked up and saw Marcie Graham holding a fairly elaborate digital Pentax. "Shooting production stills for the archives and promotion."

I held up a hand. "I'd rather you didn't," I said. Then I remembered the clause in my contract that allowed the company to use my name and my face. "Oh, what the hell."

Marcie snapped a few quick shots of us, arms around each other. "Great stuff," she said. "It'll look good in the trade papers, the composer and the ingénue."

"Ouch!" I said.

"Yeah," Jenny told her. "I'm not all that young."

"It's that whole human interest angle — composer's girlfriend wanders into stardom — a star is born." She fiddled with the lens. "Can we step inside the office for a few more? Get you guys sitting at a table looking at the script or something?"

In the office, Jenny and I sat at the worktable, an eight-by-four sheet of plywood on sawhorses that served as a central catch-all for the mounds of paper a shoot generates. Sheets stood in multicolored piles; script rewrites color-coded for everyone to pick up, piles of still photos, shooting schedules, and day-to-day task assignments.

"Pick up a schedule or something and point to it as if you're studying it."

"How's this?" Jenny said. Marcie nodded and the camera whizzed. "Do you take pictures of everybody?"

"Yeah. They're good for PR, you know, leak a few to the media. Besides, Screamer wants to see what's happening behind the scenes, not just in front of the camera, make sure they're getting their money's worth."

"Let's see how they look." I held out my hand for the camera. Marcie pushed a few buttons and gave it to me. "That button to scroll."

Marcie was a good photographer. She caught us both at flattering angles, and our smiles were genuine. "Can I get a copy of these?"

"Policy says no pictures out of our hands without studio approval, but in your case, Sam, I owe you the courtesy. Give me your e-mail address and I'll send them to you."

"That would be great. I haven't looked that good in a photograph since I was about twenty."

We all had a laugh over that, and then Simon and Anya came in.

"So, Dunne, you've graced us with your presence. Come to bid us all farewell?"

"I guess so, for a few days, at least. But as you've seen, I don't need to be here twenty-four-seven to do the score. Ed has my address in Myrtle Beach and my internet drop box. Send me the scenes. I'm working evenings, so I can spend time on the film during the day when I'm not busy ogling sweet young things on the beach." Jenny punched my arm. "Hey, I invited you along."

"We couldn't do without her this week, Sam. We're trying to wrap as much as we can before Tuscarora's management runs us out of here."

Anya pointed to Jenny. "She's been a godsend. She learns quickly and I don't have to tell her anything twice."

"And it's uncanny. Working with her is almost like working with Janine." And then Simon gave Jenny a smile and a look that made me wish I wasn't going eight hundred miles away.

XIX

I've never been much for long goodbyes, but Jenny is, so I hit the road for the Carolinas about an hour later than I anticipated and dragged a raft of mixed emotions along with me. James Taylor had it right in "Carolina in my Mind": "Peace and quiet and dogs that bite." Don't be fooled; there are always rocks under the water. When I drive a long haul, I usually set the cruise control at sixty-five and pop in an audio book. Sometimes I'll go for a favorite classic like A Tale of Two Cities or some piece of the literary canon I've missed along the way, like William Conrad's Nostromo. Other times I enjoy a really good detective thriller, one of James Lee Burke's Dave Robichaux novels or one of those gritty noir books by Max Allan Collins. It's a long way from my twenties, tooling down the Interstate at eighty-five with a quart of beer in my lap and Led Zepplin pounding the speakers through the dashboard.

This ride, I was listening to Michael Boatman read Walter Mosley's Little Scarlet. If I ever graduate beyond teaching bonehead composition as an adjunct, I want to teach a course in American Crime Fiction: Spillane, Hammet, Chandler, all the old masters through the moderns; Parker, Elroy, and definitely Mosley. I read a piece once by George Will who said that when the Old West was fenced in, the cowboys moved to town and became private eyes. That has the ring of truth for me, but at the same time, I think it speaks to a personality type that America fostered and even encouraged at the founding of the country when the land was untamed and hard men were necessary to pound it into shape. Today's genteel types recoil from such men, call them Neanderthals and haul them in front of police review boards for doing what American men have always done. Bring order to chaos. But like Jung's Shadow, the Bad Guys are never destroyed, only suppressed to ride again with new faces, and sometimes, the only true weapon against them is somebody worse. I guess life wasn't really simpler in the old days, but it was more sharply defined. As compelling as Little Scarlet was, my mind kept drifting back to the murders.

Yeah, I'd started to think of Janine's death in those terms as well as Ray's. It could have been an accident, but somebody could have switched the knives on the prop table on purpose in the hope that Janine would really die. No guarantees, but a certain expectation of success. That raised the question of who might have done it. From what Ed told me, there were plenty of motives to go around, including a big one for Simon. The publicity from Janine's death would guarantee a raft of free publicity for Lake Deadly. To quote him, "No ink is bad ink." Had he tired of his pet scream queen? Would he sacrifice her for the box office? Or would Elizabeth, who was jealous of Janine anyway? Or was it maybe Ed Leighty? Simon's failure might shake Anya loose from her slavish devotion to him and give Ed the chance he wanted. I worried about Jenny, being out there with a killer still on the loose, but at least Billings had the sense to post deputies at the camp as a security measure to keep out the curious as much as anything else, and Screamer hired a team of rent-a-cops to patrol the area at night. Jenny was still staying at our apartment, but that was no guarantee either. I'd watched Janine die with twenty people around her and a camera running. The whole thing gave me a headache. I restarted the chapter and put the whole business out of my mind for the next two hundred miles.

Pulling into Myrtle Beach is a little different from pulling into Cape May in Jersey or Lauderdale. It doesn't have that same ocean smell you find in most seashores. Maybe it's the wind. But the town is clean, the beaches are well kept, and the city fathers long ago moved any mundane businesses like hardware stores or gas stations a good half mile from the shining blue sea.

I quit counting the number of discount stores, along the highway into town, each decorated more garishly than the one before it, that hawked three dollar beach towels and five dollar aluminum chairs. There seemed to be a Ron Jon Surf Shop every three blocks. But, I reminded myself, these stores weren't somebody's hobby. If a place didn't make a profit, it would close in a week.

Joe booked me an efficiency unit for the week a block from the beach in a high rise he found online called The Breakers. Ordinarily on short notice, I'd be camped at the Holiday Inn. I was going to miss room service. Damned internet.

The first thing I noticed when I opened the door was the smell of Pine-Sol mixed with Armor All. My guess was that the cleaning ladies went over every room daily from end to end, resulting in an over-polished gloss on every smooth surface. The room felt like the Space Shuttle because the builders tried to cram what amounted to my apartment into half its space. All the kitchen hardware and cabinetry lined the right wall. Along the opposing wall across a narrow aisle was a breakfast table with a wire twist cafe chair at either end.

The general decor was as homey as a Motel 6, but unless a hurricane was brewing outside, but I guess whoever paid the tab for the week spent as little time in the place as possible. The living room featured a sofa that pulled out to a double bed at right angles to a love seat facing a flat screen TV on the wall. A door opened into the minimal bathroom that shared a wall with the kitchen and explained the narrow passage.

The bedroom had a double bed with one nightstand (no room for two), a three drawer dresser, and two big closets with mirrored doors. (Use your imagination.) I dropped my duffel bag on the floor beside the dresser and longed for LaQuinta.

I thought about calling Jenny and realized she was probably still at the camp. And her cell phone would be off while the shoot was active. So, I changed into running shoes and shorts and headed the half block to the beach to run out the kinks from driving all day. The sun was low, and the breeze was stiff, but in less than a mile, I was shaking droplets of sweat off my face with a toss of my head.

Running south, I could see the Skywheel, all two hundred feet of it turning lazily in the sunset. Below it, a changing of the guard was taking place. The last of the suntan crowd was packing up and leaving, and the late crowd, mostly families were setting up camp in the strip between the high tide line and the hotels and condo high rises that bracketed the Boardwalk.

Occasionally I heard music, most of it canned stuff from a DJ, but every so often I heard the unmistakable sound of live. I saw a crowd at tables outside a restaurant that butted right against the beach and stopped to listen. A kid about twenty-five or so in jeans and a red linen shirt was standing alone on a platform surrounded by tables. He had a bass slung over his shoulder and was playing a beat on a conga drum. He stepped back and the conga kept playing.

People have been looping, playing a riff and having it repeat electronically while building another on top of it, then another since Les Paul invented multi-track recording, but it's had a surge in popularity recently since artists like Ed Sheerhan have made it prominent again. I've used it on a song here and there with a digital delay in the past, but today's technology makes it a science. The kid played the bass a while, stepping on a button here and a button there, and soon the bass line and conga were in sync. He switched the bass for an Ovation twelve string and started the signature opening riff for "Hotel California."

The crowd caught on and there was scattered applause, and a few "oh yeahs." The kid's voice wasn't bad. He had a nice clear tenor and knew how to work it. When he got to the chorus, he kicked in a vocal harmonizer that did a creditable job. All in all, he sounded pretty good. The crowd clapped and whistled, and as people were called in for their dinner reservations, they stuffed bills in the bait bucket he kept at the edge of the stage.

He happened to look my way and I gave him a thumbs up before I set off again. Welcome to the future. I guess that kind of performance is just another consequence of the modern age. I can master a whole CD in my living room by myself with the right equipment; it's just one more step to putting the whole works on stage. I do agree with my friend jazzman Cotton Breakiron, though, when he says, "That shit puts a lot of honest people out of work."

I got to the Sky Wheel and turned around for the run back. In an hour I was showered and dressed and heading to the Boardwalk and Rollo's. Tonight was Ricky's last one before I took over, and I wanted to meet the management and eyeball the crowd.

Rollo's is one of those restaurant-bars that front the boardwalk, and being in a corner position, is open on two sides. Tables outside, tables inside and a three-sided bar lined with stools. Neon and noise. Outside, a sandwich board had my picture with the words "recording artist Sam Dunne — starting tomorrow — four nights only." I walked in just as Ricky was launching into his version of "The Breeze," a finger-picking arrangement that moved just as fast and solid as the original.

The place was packed, but I found a stool at the bar and a cute little blonde with wire rimmed glasses popped up. "What'll you have?"

"Bring me a Heineken."

"We don't have it on tap. Bottle okay?"

I nodded, studying the menu on the boards overhead. "And a cheeseburger with fries and coleslaw."

She jotted my order on a notepad and wiggled off through the gang of servers and bartenders between the bar and the kitchen. I looked around the room and saw an all-age crowd, but it was early. Mom and Dad would haul the kids away in an hour or so, and the party people would take up the slack. Somebody yelled, 'Margaritaville,' and Ricky obliged to the shouts of "Salt! Salt! Salt!" from the crowd. This gang got wound early.

The waitress brought my order and I tucked into the food like I hadn't eaten for a month.

Ricky is a big, gangly blonde-haired blue-eyed farm boy whom people like as soon as he flashes his disarming grin. He has always had the touch for working a crowd. Some people seem born for that. Their personalities sync with people from the first song, but put them in a studio, and they just can't pull it off. He had a table beside the dais where his girlfriend Doris sold his CDs, a mix of originals and covers, all recorded live and remastered to fix the blips and clinkers. It'd worked for him for twenty years; *res ipse loquitur.*

Ricky launched into "I Can't Be Bought," one of my tracks from *Requiem*, and when I looked up; he nodded at me and grinned. When the song ended, he said to the crowd, "That song, ladies and gentlemen, is the creation of the gentleman sitting right there at the corner of the bar." He pointed. "The none and only Sam Dunne, let's hear it for him." I raised a hand to wave, and the patrons hooted and whistled. Ricky went on, "Sam'll be here for the rest of the week, starting tomorrow night, so y'all come and give him a listen." More applause and Ricky launched into "Starset," one of his own.

A tall, beefy guy with the sweaty red face that portends a heart attack came up to me from the employee side of the bar. "You're Sam Dunne?" I nodded, still chewing my burger. He held out a softball sized hand to shake. "Jake Porter. I'm the manager."

I wiped the grease from my hand and shook with him. Jake cold have been forty, he could have been fifty. In the neon bar lights, his hair could have been ash blonde or ash grey. He had a pretty solid grip, which I answered with one of my own. I guessed he was an ex-jock, maybe a college football player gone to seed based on the layer of hard fat that he wore like a set of long johns under his skin.

"Tell me what I need to know."

"Start at eight, play till midnight. The system's a plug and play. We don't have a soundman, so you'll have to do your own mix from the stage. Take a break every hour or so. You have CDs to play when you're off?"

"Yeah, I have a few."

"Do you have somebody to run a merchandise table?"

"Nope, I'm on my own this trip."

"We can sell them at the register for you."

I wasn't crazy about that idea, but a pile of CDs and a box of cash on the edge of the stage was just one door too many to watch. "We can give it a try."

"Do you have T-shirts? Hats? Key chains?"

"Nope, just music."

He shrugged. "We have a family crowd early, so no raunchy stuff. After about nine-thirty, you can play whatever the party gang wants."

"Got it. Is there a place I can lock up my gear instead of carrying it back and forth? I noticed parking is a problem around here."

He nodded, "Yeah, you can —" he turned and barked at two barmaids who weren't in motion, "Hey! I don't pay you to stand still. Get on it." Back to me as if the conversation were uninterrupted, "leave your things in the storeroom. Ricky does, and we've never had a problem."

"Good enough. Can I come in the afternoon tomorrow to set up the sound?"

"Sure thing. Excuse me." Jake turned away and went back to whip cracking. And I went back to my burger.

When Ricky took his break, I joined him and Doris at his table. "Hey, Sam. Glad to see you."

"Sounding good as usual, Ricky. Looks like the crowd loves you."

He grinned. "Fooled 'em again."

"You look healthy as a horse. What's the big medical emergency?"

His face got serious. "A little bit of blockage in my colon: it's benign, but it's gotta go."

"And you'll be back in a week?"

"The miracle of micro surgery and robotics. The doc says I'll be good to go again next Monday. I just have to watch what I eat and how much. I've got the diet police here to keep me in line." He elbowed Doris who threw a French fry at him. "Can't do that next week, darlin'. I might eat it."

"All the more reason to do it now."

"I met Jake. He looks like he's about to have a stroke."

"He looks like that twenty-four-seven," Ricky said, taking a pull from his beer. "You know the type; everything's a crisis."

"And if shouting doesn't work, shout louder," Doris said.

"It must be tough acting as middleman for the owner; all responsibility and no authority."

"And that," said Ricky with an emphatic nod, "is why I stay self-employed."

When Ricky's break ended, he stood up and said, "Want to come up and do one? Kind of a teaser for tomorrow for the crowd, and a goodwill gesture for Jake?"

"Good will jester's more like it," I said. "Sure, I'll do one or two."

On the dais, standing full height, Ricky's head almost hit the ceiling. Mine didn't come so close. The platform was three feet high and cut a triangle across the boardwalk corner of the place. Passersby could look in and the stage was visible from just about anywhere inside and from all the outside tables.

Ricky handed me his Takamine and as I adjusted the strap to make up for our difference in height, he shouted, "Hey everybody! We got a superstar here, Sam Dunne. You've heard his hit LP *Requiem*, and you've heard him with Gin Sing. He's going to be here for the next four nights starting tomorrow. Let's give him a big Myrtle Beach welcome."

The crowd was drunk enough to take the bait and gave me a barrage of cheers and whistles. Ricky stepped off the stage, and I launched into the opening chord riff of "I am a Live Musician."

"Sometimes you start writing a song and it takes on a life of its own. This is one of those." The lyrics tout the virtue of playing live and solo, and the pitfalls of working with no net:

> I am a live musician, part of a dying breed.
> A microphone, a guitar and a song are all I need.
> There's lots of competition, each weekend it's a fight;
> It's karaoke, DJs and a free jukebox tonight.
> And the chorus:
> There's magic in the music in its melody and rhyme.
> I'll sing the soundtrack of your life one measure at a time.

The crowd bought the song, and I saw Jake standing behind the bar. He gave me a thumbs up. "Yeah, like Ricky said, I'll be here at Rollo's for the next four nights. Come on back and bring your friends. Here's a song you haven't heard before."

I started up the opening riff for "Let the Old Boys Play," my song about the young crowd's attitude toward veteran players:

> We got a lotta young boys with electric guitars'
> Thinkin' that they're gonna be superstars, and they
> Say it's time for rock'n'roll to turn the page.
> They want everybody with a touch of grey
> To just move over and get out of the way.
> The young'uns wanna kick the old boys off the stage.
> And the chorus:

Let the old boys play. You know they paved the way,
And without them you wouldn't have the rock'n'roll that you have today.
They got a lot to say; no matter if they're grey, You know they
Paid a lot of dues inventin' rhythm and blues — let the old boys play.

The crowd cheered and hollered, and I nodded to Ricky. He came back onstage and took the guitar from me as I said into the mic, "See you all tomorrow."

"Sam Dunne, everybody. Tomorrow night right here at Rollo's."

I left soon after and headed back to my unit. I checked my phone and saw no call from Jenny, which was no surprise. She was probably still at the camp. I punched in her number and the call went straight to voicemail, which meant her phone was off. Again, no surprise. I left her a quick message to let her know I arrived in one piece and for her to call when she got home.

I felt a little bit possessive throwing that onus on her, as if I expected her to check in with me. Whoever killed Ray McCarthy was probably three states away by then, but I was still worried about Jenny working out there.

The walk back to my room took me down Ocean Boulevard, the main drag that paralleled the beach and the Boardwalk. The sidewalks were crowded, and the traffic crawled by. In a weird juxtaposition, a boom car thumping rap music was followed three behind by a pickup truck with American and Confederate flags on poles mounted in the bed. Lots of Harleys, lots of mopeds, and lots of what looked like glorified golf carts rented by the hour but street legal.

I passed the band shell near the Sky Wheel and stopped to listen to a local blues band do a decent version of Stevie Ray Vaughn's "Pride and Joy." Better than average. And when I passed the restaurant where I'd heard the looper play "Hotel California" earlier, I heard him doing the song again. Oh well, it's early in the season, I thought. Maybe by August he'll have a whole night's worth of material.

Back at the room, I kicked off my shoes and flopped on the sofa. I don't have cable in my apartment, but the Breakers does, so I turned on the TV and surfed the channels. In five minutes, I remembered why I didn't have cable. Newton Minnow once said that television was a "giant wasteland." I think he was an optimist.

I dozed off around midnight, and the phone woke me. It was Jenny. "Hi, Sam. We just finished shooting. I'm on my way to the apartment now."

"How'd it go today?"

The sidewalks were crowded, and the traffic crawled by.

"Pretty good, but we may be moving to another location in a day or so. Screamer's getting more pressure locally to leave Tuscarora. That Ledgerton woman's fighting it, but the judge wants to be re-elected. Ed was gone all day scouting for a similar site."

"Maybe it's just as well. Tuscarora seems to have bad Karma." As I said that, I thought to myself, and Last Light Productions will probably drag it right along with the lights, cameras, and other baggage everywhere they go.

Jenny and I said goodnight soon after, and I put my phone on the charger. I adjusted the thermostat so I wouldn't freeze to death overnight in the air conditioning and climbed into bed. I closed my eyes and slept for eight hours.

XX

In the morning when I turned on my phone, there was a have-a-good-day-talk-to-you-later voice mail from Jenny and a text from Ricky Stover: "Like they say in *Star Trek*, you have the com, Sam. Adios."

The efficiency had a courtesy coffee setup, so I started the pot and sat down with my laptop and fired it up. A card on the television stand said the Breakers had free wi-fi. The network ID was simply "breakers," and the password was "guest." That should keep Homeland Security guessing for a while.

I pulled up my e-mail and found a dozen or so junk messages, and nestled among them was one from Ed Leighty. "Sam," he wrote, "I put three scenes in your drop box. Ed."

I clicked onto my drop box link and logged in. There were four new items, not three. The clips Ed sent were mpeg files. The odd one was a wmv. I double clicked on it, and while it downloaded, I poured a cup of coffee. When I sat back down at the table and saw the screen, the hand with the cup froze halfway to my mouth.

On the screen was the lake at Tuscarora, and Janine, and the knife slicing her throat. I was too stunned to stop the video and stared as the blood poured down her body. The screen went black. I stared at it for a good two minutes. Then my phone buzzed.

It was Kearny. "You heard about the video?"

"Somebody sent it to me."

"You and the world. Janine DiBasil's throat-cutting scene is all over the internet. What's the word? Viral?"

He let that sink in a minute and said, "We have the original in evidence. We gave them a copy of the rest of the scenes like you suggested, but not DiBasil's death. But there it is. Ideas?"

I thought immediately of the interview video from two days before, the copy of the footage Simon and his crew had squirreled away. Did he keep a second recording of everything as a backup? "A lot was going on at the moment. Maybe somebody dubbed the video card and put it back into the camera while everybody else was distracted by Janine's death. I don't know who or how. Jack Smith was running the camera and he was the last person I saw holding it."

I suddenly regretted pulling the power cable on the camera. It might have caught something important. "You don't think it was Schiff or his people, do you? They've got enough trouble already."

"At this point, I'm keeping an open mind."

At the back of my head, I thought again about publicity and dismissed it immediately; Janine's death was still buzzing and McCarthy's amped it up even more. Letting the video out was too soon for maximum impact, if that's what somebody wanted. "So what now?"

"Was McCarthy working the scene at the lake?"

"I can't remember right off hand. There were a lot of people at the location. He was probably one of them."

"Right now, I'm looking into whether McCarthy had access to the camera in the half hour before the posse showed up. If he had the video, maybe he tried to peddle it for getaway cash. Maybe he succeeded."

"Or blackmailed somebody with it—the mysterious knife switcher?"

"Could be. Makes as much sense as any other theory. Think about it, Sam. Let me know what you come up with." He clicked off.

My phone buzzed again. It was Jenny this time.

"You heard about the video on the internet?"

"Yeah. It showed up in my drop box. Kearny just called me about it. What's the gossip on the set?"

"Everybody's pretty freaked out about it. Did you watch it?"

"It came on before I knew what it was."

"I didn't watch it, but a lot of the crew did. Who'd put it out there for the whole world to see? I thought the cops had it."

I thought about Ed's tale of Simon's backup archive but kept my mouth shut. "As far as I know they do. Maybe someone at the precinct leaked a copy."

"But someone sent it to your drop box. That means they had your address. Do you have any idea who it might have been?"

"No, but I will find out. Maybe you ought to just go home and wait till this settles down."

"I can't, Sam. They need me today. We're on schedule now, and if we have to relocate, we'll fall behind again. I have to be here today."

"Well, be careful. I don't think this business is over yet and it won't be till Kearny catches the killer."

"I'll be careful, Sam. You be careful too. No getting eaten by a shark. I'll call you later."

She clicked off, and I wished the week were over.

The Hanniston P.D. ran a tight ship as far as evidence was concerned. I couldn't imagine Kearny and Williams letting something like that video slip by. My money was on Last Light. But why? If it was a publicity stunt, the timing was all wrong. Last Light was already on shaky ground to keep their location. As for attention, the press was still buzzing about McCarthy's murder, so there was no bump in publicity to be gained this soon.

The only thing that made sense to me was someone trying to tank the film. That took me back to the question why. And was Ray McCarthy's murder a part of the whole scenario, or was it in a separate compartment? And if Last Light had to pull out of Tuscarora, how would that affect Kearny's investigation? Right now, he had everybody in one place. If they moved out of his bailiwick, how could he and Wilson keep an eye on them all? Too many questions and no way to answer them in Myrtle Beach. Nothing to do but put in the time and wait.

I went back to my computer and clicked off the video. The other three Ed sent could wait. I really didn't feel like working with them at the moment. I clicked back to my e-mail and saw a message from Fe2O3Y on a gmail account. I hesitated to open it, but then I realized it was a nickname for Marcie based on her frizzy red hair: Rusty.

"Hi, Sam," the message read. "Here are the pictures of you and Jenny I took a few days ago. Have fun in Myrtle Beach, Marcie." Jpegs were attached. I downloaded the group and saved them onto my hard drive. Marcie was a good photographer; the pictures were sharp and well framed. One of Jenny and me arms around each other was particularly nice, and I wanted it printed and put in a frame. They were high resolution, too. I could zoom in and count the grey hairs in my beard if I wanted to, but I really didn't need that kind of reminder.

I downed the last of my coffee and headed out in search of breakfast. Two blocks away from the Breakers, I found Donovan's, a ham-and-egg diner that served breakfast all day. The place was busy, which meant the food was good, and it had no line waiting to be seated, which meant the service was good too. My kind of place. I snagged a newspaper from the counter and dropped into a booth.

In a minute, a middle-aged waitress in a white rayon uniform with "Carlotta" and a shamrock stitched in green above her breast pocket came up to the booth with a cup and saucer in one hand and a pot of coffee in the other. She was a little thick in the waist, but olive-skinned and pretty in her own way, in spite of a nose that looked as if it had been broken once. Without asking, she set down the cup and filled it.

"Ahoy, sailor. What can I bring you?"

Over her shoulder, I saw the sign for the Big Breakfast: Two eggs, waffles, and bacon. "I'll have the Big Breakfast, eggs over easy, and a pencil."

"A pencil?"

I flipped open the newspaper to the puzzle page. "Can't start the day without doing the Cryptoquote."

Carlotta laughed. She took the pencil from behind her ear and handed it to me as if she were the Lady of the Lake handing Excalibur to Arthur. "Take this one. I think I can remember your order." She hustled off and I dug into the puzzle.

The puzzle was tougher than average, a six-word, two-clause sentence, and I was nowhere near solving it when my food arrived. I was hungrier than I thought, and I shoveled it in like I was stoking a boiler.

The puzzle stumped me: Rjmu viuwmb izzbxinjmk, kouw px dp - Ibiyoiu Zbxqmy. I can usually sort them out, but this one had a few ringers in it.

First, there were no one-letter words; no easy As or Is. Second, there were no three-letter words either, which left "the," "and," and "but" out of the equation. I usually do the source name last. The puzzle makers like to quote people whose names have at least one letter that isn't in the quote. This one had two.

It was a good thing Carlotta gave me a pencil with an eraser. I tried one combination of letters, then another. I finally figured out that the last words were "to it," and that was as far as I got.

Carlotta stopped by to refill my coffee. "Stumped?"

"Yeah. I hate to admit it, but this is a tough one."

She peered over my shoulder. "You try the name yet?"

I shook my head. "Both names have a letter that doesn't show up elsewhere."

"Maybe it isn't a name." She counted the letters — "Seven and seven. If the last part of the source is six words, I try 'saying.' If it's seven, I try —"

"Proverb."

"Give it a shot." She moved to the next booth with the coffee pot.

Five of the letters in "proverb" appeared in the quotation, the E showing up four times. The P filled the double slot in the third word and the E and R fit in the second and third words. It was a pretty good chance that the first word was "when," making the first half of the sentence a dependent clause. A little noodling, and I figured out the third word: "approaches."

Blank, A, N, blank, E, R: Danger. When danger approaches. Using the I from "to it," I got "sing." When danger approaches, sing to it. A, R, A, blank, I, A, N. Arabian Proverb.

I've always been skeptical of synchronicity, but this pushed me an inch closer to the believer's pew. Carlotta walked by. "Figure it out?"

I nodded slowly. I looked up at her and said, "Do you believe in Fate?"

She thought that one over, weighing her answer. "Yeah," she said with a grin. "I believe it's your fate to leave me a big tip." And she was right.

I went back to the efficiency and opened my drop box. I clicked on the video files Ed sent and saved them onto the hard drive.

The first one was a shot of the couples sitting on a big rock on the edge of the lake passing around a bottle of wine. The guys were wearing cutoffs and T-shirts; the girls were wearing shorts and halters. Heather put a toe into the water and reached down for a handful to fling at the others. Nick pushed her in, and when she popped to the surface spluttering, the viewpoint cut to a source behind her.

Heather treaded water for a few seconds, and just under the surface, a long bony hand trailing tattered shreds of cloth brushed her calf. Heather squealed and kicked away. "Something touched me," she shouted.

"The lake's full of 'somethings,'" Nick said with a laugh. "It's probably a carp." She swam to the rock, and when Nick reached out to pull her onto it, she yanked him off balance and he fell in with her. Bobby and Jenny looked at each other and shrugged. They both jumped in too. In a minute, all four were splashing and laughing. The camera zoomed out and gave a Lake-Thing's-eye view of the swimmers. Fade to black.

The second scene was inside the tent. Jenny was changing out of her wet clothes when Bobby came in. She was already topless, and Bobby came up behind her, cupping her breasts and gently kneading them as he nuzzled her neck. Jenny closed her eyes and tilted her head back, leaning into the embrace. Robby moved around face to face with Jenny and the camera moved behind her. Robby knelt in front of her and slowly pulled down her shorts. He reached behind her and grabbed her ass with both hands and pulled her to him.

I hit Stop. Gay or not, Robby looked as if he were having a really good time. I cursed myself for getting Jenny into this in the first place, and then I cursed myself for letting jealousy get the best of me. I just had to get over it.

I hit Play. In a second or two, Nick's voice came from outside the tent. "Come on, guys. We need to get some wood together for a fire." Jenny pushed Robby away. "Later, Romeo." She reached down for her jeans, giving the camera a good look at her swaying boobs in the process. Simon knew what he wanted, all right, and he got it. I wondered whether this scene would disappear when the movie was edited but end up in Simon's private stock.

The third clip was some older footage edited into some new stuff. It was the scene Ed had described to me with the knife coming through the side of the tent and slitting the fabric in one long, smooth cut and what followed. The Lake thing, seen in silhouette against the orange fabric of the tent slithered through the slit and stood over Nick and Heather, knife in hand.

The Lake Thing's hand shot out and grabbed Nick by the throat, yanking him out of the blankets. It held him dangling while it slit his naked torso from his groin to his breastbone. Heather started awake and sat up. Before she could scream, the Lake Thing clubbed her with the butt of the knife and she fell to the side unconscious.

Nick's body shuddered and went still. The Lake Thing dropped it on the blankets and turned its attention to Heather.

The creature studied her, the camera playing over her body in the soft orange glow. Then it took her by the hair and dragged her through the slit in the tent. The slit closed behind them. The silhouettes shrank, and for a long count, the camera played the blank tent wall, then faded to black.

I had read the script at the start of the project, but it had undergone so many changes since I signed on, that I wasn't sure what I was seeing or where it fit in the time line. Simon must really have Willis dancing on this one. The whole story line seemed fluid, shifting and sliding from day to day, as if Simon were less interested in making a salable movie than he was in filming vignettes of his darkest fantasies. If the ship were going down, Simon would savor every minute before it sank, playing with his living dolls.

I shut off my laptop. Inspiration had gone someplace else.

XXI

That afternoon, I parked the van two blocks away from Rollo's, the closest space I could find, and carried in my gear. The post-lunch lull had set in, and the place was about half empty, making the house Muzak just loud enough to be annoying. There were two notes on the board. One was taped onto the top and said, "Leave the EQ drawbars as they are. They're set for the room with a pink noise machine. - Management"

The second note was a slip of paper tucked under a corner of the unit. It was in Ricky's handwriting: "Channel three is flaky; it gets loud and soft without warning." I wondered how long it had been that way. Club owners are too often content to limp along with unreliable equipment to save money in the short run, overlooking the loss of return business that comes from bad sound.

The board was a few years old, an eight-channel Crate solid state mixer/amplifier. I always preferred tube electronics myself, but we all bow to progress. My experience with solid state gear is that one failing circuit puts a drain on everything else and sooner or later brings down the whole system.

I ran an XLR cable from my amp into the board. I prefer that to a direct box because I can hear the actual sound of the guitar behind me, not just what comes out of the monitors and the house system. Also, I know what to tweak to accommodate the room, and it's within reach.

I plugged in my guitar, tuned it, and set it in its stand. Then I stepped off the stage and walked over to the bar. One of the barmaids hustled over. "Can you turn off the music while I do a sound check?"

"I'll go ask Jake." She disappeared into the kitchen and in a minute Jimmy Buffet stopped in mid chorus.

A little fiddling with the knobs and drawbars gave me a good approximation of my amp sound through the whole system. When the music stopped, the customers didn't seem to mind. Rather than annoy them with a lot of aimless noodling, I ran through a fingerpicking solo version of Bob Dylan's "Don't Think Twice, It's All Right." A little less mid and a tad more bass and my guitar was pretty much where I wanted it.

Time to EQ the mic. Instead of saying the usual, "Test—one, two, three" or "Check—one, two," I sing an *a cappella* line or two from a song. After all, I'd be singing through the mic, not talking through it. I sang the opening lines from "Peaceful Easy Feeling." The system was bass heavy, probably set for Ricky's voice, and one adjustment made the second line sound better than the first. I picked up my guitar and played the song end to end. There was even a little bit of applause when it ended. "Thank you folks," I said with a nod. "I'll be back tonight at eight." By the time I had my guitar back in the carry bag, Jimmy Buffet was back.

I sat at the bar and ordered a beer. Jake came out wearing the same clothes and the same sheen of sweat he'd had on the night before. "Everything okay?"

I nodded. "It all works."

"Then I'll see you tonight," he said turning away.

"Eight o'clock," I said to his retreating back. Personality was definitely not his long suit.

The best thing about playing at the beach is, well, the beach. Myrtle Beach is more an area for families than frat boys. Most of the shore is wall to wall blankets and umbrellas. I threw down my towel close to the surf. I put on plenty of sun block — don't want to work with a sunburn — and flopped down with a Carl Hiaasen novel.

There's something therapeutic about the seashore. Maybe it's the steady pulse of the waves, almost hypnotic, or the unshaded sun that puts life on hold for a while. It was about three in the afternoon, and life wasn't looking too bad.

A middle-aged couple sat beside me in those low-to-the-ground webbed beach chairs. The woman set the tabloid she was reading beside her chair and I got a look at the cover. It was the latest issue of *Nightside*, and there was my face and Janine DiBasil's on the cover under the bold headline "The Sam Dunne Jinx? — Death on the Set."

I stared at it for a minute, and when I looked up, the woman was looking down at me. Did she recognize me? I felt like an insect wriggling on a pin. Then she said, "Did you want to read that? I'm finished with it."

"Uh, yeah, sure, thanks," I mumbled.

"Just please don't do the crossword puzzle. I always save them for Bob." She tilted her head to her husband dozing under a ball cap. Half of me wanted to read the story, and the other half wanted to bury it in the sand beside my towel. The masochistic side of me won the battle, and I turned to the article, sandwiched between a rumor about a legal battle over Michael Jackson's remains and the latest Kardashian eruption.

Text and photos spread across two pages of the tabloid: a picture of me in the deputy costume and an old one of me with Gin Sing; a triptych of Danny Barton, Eddie Shay, and Lottie Williams, each with an R.I.P. caption above the face, and a shot of Janine DiBasil masked with strategically placed black tape beside a blurred snapshot of Ray McCarthy. And there was Wendy Conn, looking very serious. Under her picture was the caption: Reporter says, "I was there. He almost got us all killed."

The text followed the usual tabloid format. It began with the question as statement in bold type: Does death follow certain people around, striking others down but leaving them unscathed?

The article went on, in smaller print, reading like the teaser blurb from the dust jacket of a book. "Recording artist turned actor Sam Dunne seems to be one of those, having been present on the set when a beautiful young starlet met a grisly death; one of the crew was found dead a few days later. But Janine DiBasil and Ray McCarthy are only two of the people from Dunne's immediate circle of acquaintance to meet violent deaths within the last two years. He may have personally killed only one of them, Danny Barton, but the jinx that follows him may have led the others to the Reaper as well.

"Sam Dunne is no gang-banger, no drug-dealer, no hard-core rapper; he's an aging rock guitarist turned actor, whose proximity to dying people looks to be more than coincidental." I was amazed that Wendy got Ray McCarthy's murder in the piece. She must have had the story ready to go the day I saw her at the set talking with Simon and Elizabeth and scared up the photo somehow. The miracle of electronic journalism.

The article was typical tabloid stuff, although written a notch higher in quality than you might expect to find in a scandal rag. It recounted the gory details of Janine's accident, and it was obvious that Wendy had watched the clip. I made a mental note to mention that to Kearny. Ray McCarthy's death was next, which was being investigated as a homicide. Again, the unanswered questions; I could almost hear Leonard Nimoy's voice from the old *In Search Of* TV series. "Is there a connection between Janine DiBasil's ghastly accident and Ray McCarthy's alleged murder? Was the starlet's accident really a hideous mishap, or was it murder too?"

More after these messages, I thought.

"But a violent end is no stranger to Sam Dunne, as witnessed by the deaths of three of his acquaintances just two years ago." What followed was, more or less, a synopsis of Wendy's book *Dead Man's Melody* (she managed to mention the title three times), recounting the deaths of Eddie, Lottie, and Danny, and attributing them to what she called "the mysterious malediction that seems to follow Dunne around like a second shadow lurking under his own."

She wrapped it up with her trump card, reprising her book and accusing me of recklessly baiting Danny into the shootout and nearly getting her and Kearny killed. "The film continues shooting as you read this," Wendy wrote. "Death comes in threes, as the superstition goes; three died in the Gin Sing incident; already two are dead on the set of *Lake Deadly*. Who will be the third to fall to the Sam Dunne jinx?"

Next to me, the woman who gave me the paper was folding her chair. I sat up and held the *Nightside* issue out to her. "Thanks, ma'am."

She smiled, and then she said in a voice too low for Bob to hear. "You should keep it. For what it's worth, you don't look cursed to me." She winked and left me staring after her as she and Bob ambled past the life guard tower to their time-share.

Not exactly what I expected, but it all made sense. Simon and Last Light got a pass from Wendy because she was going to do the documentary with him and tie it into her next book. I could imagine her in the film, sitting at a desk in front of an impressive wall of books, her glasses a little down her nose so she could look over the lenses at the interviewer. She could paraphrase her famous line to me from *Dead Man's Melody*: He dances with a couple of toes over the edge all the time, even when somebody's holding his hand to get pulled over with him. He's dangerous.

Maybe so, Wendy, but Danny's in the ground, and you aren't.

I checked my phone. No calls from Jenny. No texts from Jenny. I went onto Facebook to see whether she'd left anything there. I had opened a Facebook page at Joe Mancini's insistence, but I never seemed to have the time to devote to really making it work for me. I posted my gig schedule, and a few photos, but that was about it. I'm still trying to figure out Twitter.

There were no messages for me. I clicked onto Jenny's page and saw she had put up a photo album of shots from the set. I scrolled through them. As far as I could tell, they were all stills that Marcie had shot, probably chosen and authorized by Elizabeth, who seemed to be in charge of public relations. They all looked pretty tame compared to the movie footage, but I guess T&A pictures are still a no-no on Facebook. Eight photos, and I wasn't in any of them.

I suppose there's a marketing strategy behind that. The droolers who'll pay to see *Lake Deadly* don't want to see the star hooked up with another guy, especially one old enough — let's face it — to be their father. It spoils the fantasy. I made a mental note to myself to put the picture of Jenny and me holding each other on my Facebook page. As for use permission, Last Light could kiss my ass.

Jenny and I have never been possessive with each other. In both our jobs, we get a lot of flirting and a lot of temptation, but we've always had the sense that anytime one of us goes away, he or she will always come back. Today, I felt like Jenny was past the breakwater, and the movie was pulling her farther than she could swim back on her own. I sent her a text: Miss you. Let me know how it's going.

XXII

Back in the efficiency, I showered and shaved. I felt a little sting across my shoulders from the hot water; I got more sun than I imagined. Tomorrow, I thought, I'll have to get some food in the fridge so I don't bankrupt myself eating in restaurants. I dressed and slung my guitar over my shoulder, opting to walk to Rollo's instead of fighting for a parking space or risking a ticket when the meter ran out.

The sidewalks and the Boardwalk were crowded, and at the bandshell, I saw a guy dressed as Elvis doing a karaoke act. He was standing in the courtyard in front of the stage beside an open guitar case to collect tips. The guitar was nowhere in sight, and I suspect he brought the case with him empty. A gaggle of blue-haired ladies clustered around him and threw dollars into the case like horny housewives at a Chippendale's show.

I respect anyone who will get up and perform, but this guy strained the limits. When he couldn't reach notes in the song, he spoke the lyrics. I found out later that he's a local real estate broker who's some big wheel in town and who uses his clout to book himself on the Boardwalk a couple of nights a week all summer. I guess being in the spotlight is irresistible to some people.

Rollo's was packed, inside and out, and the servers were scurrying. I went into the storage area to tune up, away from the Muzak and ran into Jake coming out. "Good. You're here already. I get hives when people show up five minutes before show time."

I laughed. "Relax, Jake. You'll live longer."

"Give me the high sign when you're ready to start, and I'll shut off the music."

"You got it."

Every time I climb the stage to play a new place, I feel a certain sense of anxiety, but it evaporates as soon as I start playing. I've got an act to sell, and I'm going to sell it with everything I've got.

"Hello, Myrtle Beach. I'm Sam Dunne. Who wants to have fun?"

The crowd hooted and whistled, and we were off.

I launched into "After the Sun Comes Up," and followed it with "One Finger in Ten," then the requests started. The crowd was used to Ricky, I guess, and they were calling out songs one after the other. Ricky kept a white board on the stage under the mixer table, and I scrawled the songs on it, enough for a whole set.

"I'll try to get all of them for you," I said, "and if I don't know the song you asked for, I'll play one that sounds like it."

The night went fast. It was half over before I got through the first wave of requests, mixed in with my own material. I knew all of the requested songs but three, and for two of those I was able to pull lyrics and chords from the Internet on my tablet. I took a break at ten, and put on my CD. "I used to put up a sign that said, 'take me home with you: ten bucks, but people kept getting the wrong idea. If you like what you hear, CDs are ten dollars at the register. I'll be back in a few minutes."

I pulled a wad of bills out of the Mason jar I use for tips and ambled over to the bar to order a beer. Someone tugged at my sleeve. "Hey, Sam." It was a thirty-something with a sunburned nose and a skimpy halter. "Sign your CD for me."

"Sure, darlin'," I said. She handed me a copy of *Requiem* and a pen. "What's your name?"

"I'm Mandy, but I'm buying it for my husband. Make it out to Chuck."

"Yes, ma'am." I scrawled a dedication on the disc, autographed it and handed it back. "There you go." I signed three more of them before I finished my beer and went back onstage. The evening was turning out to be fun. The crowd was rowdier when I came back on, the family contingent gone.

I caught their mood and came on with "The Idea Song":

Maybe it wasn't such a good idea for you to dial 911
When your husband came home early, and he pulled out a gun.
And maybe it wasn't such a good idea for you to have him thrown in jail.
He's gonna do his worst, my wife don't get first as soon as he makes bail.
Seemed like a good idea at the time.
Even though it seemed a little bit out of line.

Any time your bad idea lines up with mine,
Seems like a good idea every time.

The crowd made so much noise that people walking past on the Boardwalk stopped to see what was going on and soon a crowd was gathered outside. People were two deep at the bar. Jake climbed onto the stage behind me and turned up the volume on the sound system.

"If you can't find a chair tonight, come on back tomorrow. I'll be here all week."

The second half of the night went faster than the first. It was midnight, and I did two encores before I shut down. I sold all the CDs I brought in but two, and the tips were generous. Like I said, Rollo's was my kind of place.

The Boardwalk was still crowded when I walked back to the Breakers, and when I got onto Ocean Boulevard, the traffic had thinned out quite a bit. Time to eat.

Skippy's across from the Ripley's Believe it or Not Museum looked like a good place to drop anchor. It was a beer and burger joint whose specialty was a foot long chili dog with Pepper Jack cheese and jalapenos. Heartburn on a long bun. I opted for a cheeseburger and sweet potato fries with a draft on the side. At my age, coffee at midnight is a sure prescription for insomnia.

The waitress took my order and while I waited, I checked my phone. Three calls: one from Jenny, one from Joe, and one from Kearny.

Jenny's call came at ten-thirty. "Hi, Sam. Simon and Elizabeth told us all that we're pulling out of Tuscarora tomorrow and moving to a place called Lost Creek, West Virginia to finish filming." I knew before Jenny said it what was coming next. "It's too far to drive back and forth, especially at night in the mountains, so I'm going to have to stay there until we finish. I'm going to bed now, but I'll have my phone on tomorrow since we won't be shooting. Call me. Miss you a bunch, Sam."

I hit the tab to replay the message just to hear Jenny's voice again. Okay, I'm sentimental. So what?

Joe's call came right after midnight. He said to call him back regardless of the hour. I figured he wanted to see how the gig went at Rollo's, counting his money in advance. I sent him a text and told him he could order his Mercedes. He texted me back: Call me.

"What's up, Joe?"

"I got a call from Eddie Bates at the Pyramid. He said some ASWI

I checked my phone…three calls.

agent named Whitey Dixon was leaning on him, and he and his partner dropped your name as the reason. I got the same call from Mike Pierce at the La-Ja Lounge yesterday. What'd you do to piss those people off?"

"Nothing special. I just pulled the plug on their shakedown at Mike and Kelli's, and they got a less than cordial reception from the goombahs at Dunningstown Inn, which was probably my fault. I guess they took it personally." I thought of Whitey pointing his finger at me.

"Yeah? Well somebody's painted a bull's eye on your back."

"I don't know why they'd bother with the Pyramid. I played there twice two years ago and haven't been back since."

"Looks like they're using the old IRS trick; they're going back through past newspaper ads to see where you've been and using that to frame their agenda. This is going to hurt you and me if word gets around that you drag trouble behind you."

"Oh, you've seen *Nightside*." Silence. "I have an idea how to deal with those ASWI bloodsuckers, Joe. What do you say we round a couple more singer-songwriters and set up gigs where we each play all originals for an hour for some base pay and set up a table to sell our CDs? The bar owners would turn a crowd and ASWI couldn't touch them."

"If you can find two or three other performers who aren't afraid to buck them, and club owners willing to take the risk."

"We'll talk about it when I get back. In the meantime, relax. You ought to come down to Myrtle. Kick back; cop a tan."

"You make my teeth hurt."

"Here comes my food. I'll call you tomorrow." I decided I'd let Kearny's call wait. No sense ruining my appetite unnecessarily, even if it meant indigestion after the fact.

After I finished eating, I ordered another beer and punched in my voicemail code. Kearny's message was tagged at eight thirty. It was short and simple. "There've been some interesting developments. I need to know what you know. Call me."

I figured whatever it was, it could keep till morning. I shut off my phone and went back to my beer.

XXIII

woke the next morning to thunder. It was pouring rain outside my window. I pulled on a T-shirt, ran a brush through my hair and wished I had an umbrella as I hustled the two blocks to Donovan's.

Carlotta walked past my booth and threw me a bar towel. "You're dripping on the formica." She came back with a coffee cup and the pot. She threw down a section of the newspaper. "Saved you a puzzle page."

"Thanks."

She took the pencil from behind her ear and set it on the paper. "This is getting to be a habit. What can I bring you?"

"Why mess with success? Bring me the Big Breakfast."

"Eggs over easy, right?"

"You have a good memory."

"Keeps 'em coming back." She turned and started for the kitchen then stopped and said over her shoulder, "You sounded pretty good last night, Sam. Not bad for somebody my age."

"You were at Rollo's?"

"Yeah, believe it or not, I do have a life outside this place."

At least she didn't recognize me from the cover of *Nightside.*

The Cryptoquote was a little easier than the day before. The nine-letter, one-word attribution had letter placement that let me know it wasn't Aristotle, so it was likely Anonymous. A four letter contraction with an O for the second letter gave me the T. By the time Carlotta set down my plate, I had it solved: "See what the others don't see. This is creativity. - Anonymous"

The same could be said for detection. I wondered if Kearny ever tackled puzzles in his spare time.

"Another meaningful message?" Carlotta refilled my coffee.

"Maybe. I guess they're all meaningful to one degree or another, or nobody would repeat them."

She moved down the row of booths with the coffee pot and left me to think. What did I see? Anything that the others didn't? Worth thinking about, but not till after I finished my coffee. My phone buzzed in my pocket. It was Kearny again. I let it go to voicemail. He could wait fifteen minutes.

Carlotta brought the check and I pulled out a wad of tip jar singles, counting them out on the table. "If I didn't know better, I'd think you were a male stripper." She laughed. "But then again, if you had a lot of fives and tens mixed in, I'd think you were a really good male stripper."

"If only," I said, laughing with her.

"Come back and see us again, Sam," she said, and paused just a beat too long before she said, "Soon."

I went back to the efficiency and pulled up Kearny's number on the cell phone. He answered on the second ring. "I know you're busy, being a celebrity on the cover of *Nightside* and all. Glad you could find the time to call me back."

"You called at ten o'clock. I can't answer the phone when I'm onstage, and when I was done, I figured you might sleep at night like normal people do. What's up?"

"Did you know that Last Light Productions is ready to tits up? Chapter eleven?"

"Wouldn't know it by me," I said. "The last check they wrote me went through okay."

"Seems that they're in financial difficulty and *Lake Deadly* is their last hope. If it bombs, they go down the chute with it. Suggest anything to you?"

"You're the detective. You tell me."

"I'm thinking that somebody wants the whole line of dominoes to fall; the movie, the company, and Schiff. Who'd want that?"

I thought of Jerry's remark about job and paycheck. "Nobody from the movie. It's a living for them."

"Except maybe Elizabeth. They have liability death and injury coverage on all their people, which you'd expect, but Last Light is a beneficiary on a rider that covers their potential inconvenience and expense at the loss of a star in the middle of filming. Janine DiBasil's parents get a hundred grand, and so does Last Light."

"That sounds crazy."

"I thought so too, until I found out that Miley Cyrus's tongue is insured for a million bucks. More to the point, Daniel Craig's body is insured for nine-and-a-half mil because he does his own stunts, and if he's hurt or killed on the set it could tank a fifty-million dollar film. So, Janine DiBasil is worth a hundred large to Last Light — if her death was a production-related accident."

"And if it wasn't?"

"Last Light gets zip."

"So, you're saying somebody at Last Light might've set up Janine's death to look like an accident to collect the payout. But where does Ray McCarthy fit into all this?"

"Maybe he sharpened the knife. Maybe he switched it for the dull one, or maybe he just saw something and after he had to run, he tried a squeeze play for quick cash and got himself killed."

"Who do you like for it?"

"I have a few people in mind, but the top two are Schiff and his wife. They would benefit most from the windfall."

"I think Simon's ego is too big for him to scuttle one of his masterpieces."

"But it does give a new twist to 'Director's Cut.' Money talks."

The documentary made more sense to me now than ever, and so did moving to a new location. It would stall having to pay Tuscarora, and it would take them out of Kearny's immediate reach. "I heard they're pulling out of Tuscarora. How'll that affect your investigation?"

"It won't make it any easier. I can't hold thirty people on suspicion of murder without some kind of probable cause. Besides, they all have alibis. The night of McCarthy's murder, the photographer, the girl he tried to rape?"

"Marcie Graham?"

"Yeah, her. She took pictures of everybody that night around the time McCarthy was killed. Everybody was gathered around the campfire. That accounted for most of them. And she seems to have all the others covered; Schiff and his wife in a meeting with that Willis character. Leighty and Savage working in the office.

"On another issue, Last Light's lawyer, that Ledgerton woman got Hunter permission to leave the county. I didn't expect the judge to make him stay. The whole community wants them gone."

"There's something else I heard, and in the light of the company's shaky finances, it makes more sense now than ever." I told him about the documentary, the backup footage, and Wendy Conn's participation.

When I finished, Kearny didn't say anything long enough for me to ask, "Still there?"

"How long have you known about this, Sam?"

"I just found out," I lied. "I guess they've been working on it on the sly since Janine's accident."

"Still won't call it murder, huh?"

"No, but I'm getting closer every day."

After Kearny's call, I needed a few minutes to think before I called Jenny. How desperate were Simon and Elizabeth? Enough to kill somebody to save their company? The insurance money was one angle, the publicity another. Income from the documentary might be their savior. According to Ed, Elizabeth hated Janine, but did she hate her enough to want her dead? And I couldn't imagine Simon, as fixated as he was with Janine, going along with a plot to kill her.

Who else? The rest of the cast and crew needed the production to continue so they'd be paid. Maybe McCarthy: he was a psycho, but then who killed him? Was he in on it with someone else? I was glad it was Kearny's mess to deal with and not mine.

I punched in Jenny's number and she answered on the third ring. "Sam! It's good to hear your voice. How's the weather down there?"

"Raining hard, but it can't last. How's it going for you?"

"Everybody's been packing and loading. We're leaving Tuscarora today to set up at the new site. I'll be staying in a motel with the rest of the cast and crew."

"Make sure the manager isn't a taxidermist."

She laughed and hesitated before she spoke again. "Good news and bad news, Sam: the bad news is that Screamer changed their mind about the CGI. The good news is that Simon's going to reshoot Janine's scenes with me and I'll get star billing — and a raise."

And an insurance policy? That hit me like a douse of ice water. It didn't take me long to see that there never was going to be any CGI. Simon had this bait and switch planned all along.

I was silent too long. "Sam? Are you still there?"

"Yeah. I'm still here."

"You're not happy." She sounded defensive.

"It's not that. You don't need my permission, or even my approval. I'm happy you've gotten this break, but I'm pissed off at the way Simon's manipulated all of us. And I've seen the way he looks at you when he thinks nobody's watching. You're his new Janine DiBasil. And you remember how she ended up."

"It's not like that, Sam." Jenny was getting an edge in her voice. "He's never said a word out of line to me."

"He doesn't have to. He's posing you in front of the camera and giving you orders like some high-priced fetish model to act out his fantasies. Has he offered you another picture after this one's done?"

She didn't answer for a while. "I thought you'd be glad I got this chance. It's one in a million."

"'I thought that you'd want what I want; sorry, my dear. . . . Send in the clowns.'" It was a knee jerk reaction, and I was sorry as soon as I said it.

"You've had your moment of glory, Sam. Why don't you want me to have one of my own?"

"Jenny, I—," I couldn't finish the sentence.

Now it was her turn to give me the silent treatment. I finally said, "I think maybe we'd better take a step back and talk about this another time soon."

"Suits me," she said, and she was gone. I wished more than ever that I wasn't eight hundred miles away. The thought of Simon making Jenny a part of his collection wasn't improbable. I thought of John Derek, who replaced Linda Evans with Ursula Andress and then Ursula with Bo, all variations on the same woman. And now that Janine was gone, Jenny was taking her place.

That threw suspicion back at Simon. I thought of Janine's disdain for him. Had the twisted bastard tired of her? Was he warped enough to want Janine gone so he could replace her with a new, naive starlet? And what would he do when he tired of Jenny?

It was still raining too hard for a run on the beach, so I pulled up the scenes Ed had sent me the day before. Watching them now and knowing that Jenny's face would be on the screen along with the rest of her put it all in a different perspective. It was as if putting her face out there was more indecent than showing her body. It was irrational, it was unprofessional, but I couldn't help the way I felt.

I wanted to call her back, try to talk this out, but I knew that would only make things worse. All things considered, it was probably better that I was in Myrtle Beach, where I couldn't get my hands around Simon Schiff's throat.

XXIV

The rain quit, so I walked to Rollo's at seven. The Boardwalk was wall-to-wall again. Myrtle Beach's boardwalk is different from Wildwood or Ocean City. Those two have big piers with amusement park rides and shill games from end to end. Myrtle Beach's boardwalk is short by comparison and has more restaurants and gift shops than anything else. The amusement rides are a mile or so away in a special entertainment complex that covers three city blocks, making the Boardwalk more casual, less frenetic.

Rollo's was busy already, and as soon as I walked in, Judy, one of the servers, waved me over. "Jake wants to see you. He's in the back." I threaded my way around the tables to the door to the storeroom and found the door to the office open.

I walked in and the first thing I saw was the cover of *Nightside* on Jake's desk.

"You give me heartburn, Dunne." He prodded a meaty finger at the tabloid. "Why didn't you tell me about this?"

"Because I didn't know it was coming till I saw it myself. Besides, what does it change?"

"You better hope nothing. If you cost me business over this crap, there'll be hell to pay."

I grinned. "Who knows? Maybe you ought to put the front page out on the marquee next to my name, now that I'm famous."

Jake glared at me. "Don't bring it up from the stage. You got that?"

"Sure. I got it. Now if you'll excuse me, I have to tune up. I'm on in fifteen minutes."

I could feel Jake's eyes boring into my back as I walked away, but at that moment, he was the least of my concerns.

The second night went as well as the first. The crowd was good, and Jake was making money. When I took my first break, a big guy in a ball cap that said "Still Single, Ladies" asked me to sign a CD. I did, and then he said, "And my wife asked me to get you to sign this." He handed me a copy of *Nightside*.

I hesitated for a second then thought about Simon's comment: no publicity is bad publicity. "How do you want me to make it out?"

Back onstage I scanned the crowd. I was looking for Carlotta and found her sitting at the bar. She was talking to some guy in a biker vest. I couldn't catch her eye, so I let it go. I also found Whitey. He was sitting at a back table with two other men. The big-haired broad was nowhere to be seen, so this probably wasn't a business call.

One of his pals wore a sweatshirt with the sleeves cut off at the armpits to show off a pair of bodybuilder arms, and the other, a man with a leaner build more like a boxer than a wrestler, wore a black fedora and a Hawaiian shirt with orchids. I've been around enough to know leg-breakers when I see them.

They stayed at the table till a quarter to twelve when the muscle boys stood up and walked out. Whitey stayed put. I took my guitar to the storeroom and saw Jake back in the office.

"I saw some boys from ASWI out front. They give you any grief?"

He looked up from a pile of receipts. "Hell, no. I pay those vultures at BMI every six months, like every club and restaurant up and down the Boardwalk. I don't know what they're doing here."

I nodded. "Just wondering." I went back to the storeroom and laid my guitar on a high shelf. I unzipped its Kevlar carry case and stuffed some tablecloths in it to plump it out to the right shape. Then I stepped behind the bar. South Carolina is one of the few eastern states that doesn't have carry permit reciprocity with Pennsylvania. I had unloaded my Beretta and locked it in the console of my van before I crossed over from North to South Carolina, so I had to make do with the aluminum baseball bat propped beside the beer cooler. I picked it up when no one was looking, held it at my side, and slipped back into the storeroom.

The bat fit nicely down the center of my guitar bag, held in place by the padding. I left the zipper about halfway down, slipped an arm through one of the shoulder straps and walked out. I couldn't see Whitey, but I was sure he was watching me.

A couple of blocks down Ocean Boulevard, I caught sight of the big guy in the sweatshirt behind me, reflected in a shop window and figured his buddy was somewhere up ahead. I crossed Ocean and took a parallel street, more an alley with no sidewalk, a little less lit and almost deserted. Two blocks further, I heard feet behind coming up behind me.

I pulled out the bat. Sweatshirt was moving for me, planning to tackle me from behind and running too fast to stop. I swept the bat through his ankles, taking him off his feet. The boxer came from the other direction and tried kidney punching me, but the tablecloths in the carry bag got in the way and padded the blow. I swung the bat like a golf club and brought it up between his legs. He doubled over and I swatted him across his lower back. He'd be pissing blood for a week.

I shucked off the bag. Sweatshirt was on his feet again, a little wobbly but still game. He started at me with his fists up. I swung for the bleachers at his head. He twitched back, but I stepped into the swing at the last second, and the tip of the bat caught him on the left side of his jaw. Blood and teeth flew. I raised the bat to finish him off. That's when an orange curtain fell around me, and I flopped on the pavement like a fish on the dock.

If my mind and body were working at the moment, I would have recognized Whitey standing over me with a taser in his hand. His voice seemed to come down a long, empty tunnel. "Think you're one smart sumbitch, don't you, Dunne. Well, you're gonna find out right now what happens when you get bright with me." He kicked me a good one in the ribs and a glancing shot to the face with the metal toe plate of his Tony Lama boots, but he was wasting his time. I didn't even feel it.

My arms were splayed out like Christ on the cross. He put one boot on my wrist and raised the other to stomp my fingers with that hard stacked heel. "We're gonna find out how well you play left-handed guitar, smart boy." I thought about rolling over and ripping off his balls with my free hand, but the notion just floated away.

"One, two. Aaaugh!" Whitey screamed and clawed at his face. I've been maced a few times in my life, and it's one smell you never forget. Carlotta sprayed him again, giving him a good shot up his nose and down his choking throat.

"Fire! Fire!" She shouted. She got sweatshirt in the eyes. In a few seconds, doors opened, lights came on, and people spilled into the alley. Whitey and his pals took off seconds ahead of the sound of sirens. When the cops arrived, Carlotta was holding me across her lap like Michelangelo's *Pieta*.

I was lucky. Carlotta knew one of the cops and convinced him that she was walking home and ran across me getting mugged. When they asked her about the bat, she shrugged and said it must have been theirs. He was skeptical, but I suppose he hated unnecessary paperwork as much as the next policeman.

"Come on," she said, putting a shoulder under my armpit. "They'll give us a lift to my place." I was in no shape to argue. "Besides," she whispered, "What'll you do if they're waiting for you back at your room?"

I remember climbing a flight of stairs and being led down a hallway to a bed that felt like heaven. I remember hands pulling off my shoes and pulling a blanket up to my chin.

"I, I —,"

"Shh. Tomorrow."

And that's the last thing I knew till morning.

I woke up feeling like they'd used the bat on me, not the other way around. I could barely turn my head to the right. The taser had locked up my muscles so tight that the right side of my neck and my chest would barely move. The bedside clock read five-fifteen. I could hear a shower running down the hall. I tried to sit up and flopped back down on the bed, my head almost exploding.

The shower shut off, and in a minute, the bathroom door opened framing Carlotta wrapped in a towel, her dark hair hanging to her shoulders in damp ringlets. "I'll give you a minute to take inventory before I ask how you're doing."

She turned her back and took off the towel, rubbing it in her hair. On her left shoulder, I saw a tattoo, a Zodiac symbol. "What's your sign?"

She looked over her shoulder and smiled. "I ought to be insulted if that's the first thing you noticed. I'm a Virgo."

She laughed and I laughed till I felt a jolt in my ribs. "I'll take your word for it." She stepped out of sight and came back in a bra and panties. "I have to go to work in a few minutes. You can stay here as long as you need to; just lock up if you leave before I get back."

"Carlotta, how did you end up in the middle of that?"

"Truth? I went to Rollo's to see you, maybe get you to buy me a beer, maybe lure you back here. Looks like I got my wish." She pulled her uniform over her head.

"You always carry mace?"

"Those bums were lucky I wasn't in my car. I carry a can of Easy Off oven cleaner under the seat."

"Jesus. Remind me to never piss you off. Why'd you yell 'fire?'"

"If you yell 'help,' nobody wants to get involved. If you yell 'fire,' everybody comes running, 'cause they don't know which way the wind's blowing." She leaned over the bed and studied my face. "I'd kiss you, but I can't see a place that doesn't hurt."

I squeezed her hand. "Carlotta, all I can say is thanks."

She nodded and headed for the door. She stopped and turned back toward me. "So, do you believe in Fate yet, Sam?"

I heard the outer door close, and I shut my eyes. Then I realized I hadn't called Jenny. I pulled out my cell phone and lit it up. No calls. Five thirty. It was too early to call Jenny, and at the same time, maybe it was too late.

My bladder felt like it was going to burst. I eased myself over the side of the bed and half staggered to the bathroom. The makeup lights over the medicine cabinet mirror made my eyes hurt, so I fumbled for the light switch and turned on the dark. I barked my shin on the bed frame finding my way back, but compared to my other hurts, it rolled off me. I dropped onto the bed and slipped into unconsciousness.

XXV

When I woke, Carlotta was sitting on the bed beside me.

"What time is it?"

"Three-thirty. Are you hungry?"

"Now that you mention it, yeah."

"I'll see what I have in the fridge." She looked me over top to bottom. "You need a shower. There are clean towels on the shelf over the john."

I stood under the hottest water I could stand for five minutes to loosen my stiff muscles, then the coldest for another two or three. I toweled off, careful to avoid the hand sized black and blue bruise over my ribs. I looked in the mirror and saw the start of a shiner under my left eye. I was lucky. If Whitey had better aim, he could have broken my cheekbone or worse.

I pulled on my clothes and stepped out of the bathroom. I don't know why more restaurants haven't figured it out, but breakfast smells good any time of day. Carlotta was stirring a skillet full of eggs, sausage, cubed potatoes and peppers. She had changed into cutoff jeans and a red tank top. Her hair was pulled back into a bushy tail. "You look human again, Sam. Coffee's ready; get a cup from the drain board."

I poured some for myself and sat at the dinette table. Sunlight streamed through the window beside me, and made the whole scene look so pleasant I could almost believe the ugliness of the night before was just a bad dream. At least I could till I shifted my weight and got a stab from my ribs.

Carlotta shoveled the scramble onto plates and set them on the table. "You want Tabasco sauce for the eggs?" I shook my head. "Anything else?"

I laughed. "Sit down and eat. You're off duty, remember?"

"Old habits die hard." She set two white pills beside my coffee. "Coated aspirin. Five hundred milligrams. Take them with the food."

"Yes, Ma'am." I was hungrier than I thought, and it didn't take me long to empty my plate.

"You want more coffee?" She went for the pot before I could answer. She poured another cup for us both and said, "Let's take it out on the balcony."

The balcony was on the shade side of the building and barely had enough room for two canvas sling chairs and a table. The view wasn't exactly inspiring, an identical apartment building across the alley. Away from the tourist corridor, life looked pretty much the same in a vacation town as everywhere else.

"So," I said. "Tell me about Carlotta."

"Not much to tell." She tucked her legs under her and took a sip of her coffee. "I was born here and never left. Married a local, and he punked out on me after two kids."

I reached over and brushed the side of her nose with my forefinger. "He give you that?"

"Naah." She laughed. "Believe it or not, I got it falling off my bicycle when I was eight years old. Donnie never hit me because he knew I'd knock him on his ass if he did. He just left, and I entered the service industry at the tender age of twenty. I've been waitressing ever since. When you grow up in a vacation spot, you learn how to play the game early.

"People think waitressing leads to a broken home; it's really the other way around. Broken homes lead to waitressing. And now, the kids are grown and gone, but the job is still there."

"Must be tough hauling yourself out of bed at five every morning."

"Not as tough as working nights. I made more in tips working the late turn in restaurants, but it grinds you down. There's no more stressful job in the world than making sure everybody else is having a good time. In a vacation town, they're on the Jones twenty-four-seven. At the end of the night there's a vacuum; where do you go for some fun of your own? You end up on a stool in some after-hours bar with all the other waitresses, bartenders and busboys. I bet you know all about it."

"Amen. It can beat you up if you let it. Not to sound egotistic, but I've reached a point that I don't play a bad gig; sometimes I get a bad crowd. If they aren't into what I'm doing, so what. I know guys who let that drag them down, but I won't let other people run my emotions. Nights when I see they aren't buying it, I play what I want, and entertain myself."

"Didn't Ricky Nelson sing about that?"

I laughed. "'Garden Party'. You know your pop music"

"I ought to. It's been the sound track of my life for twenty years playing over my shoulder in one place after another." She looked away from me, up at the sky over the roofline across the street. Her face hardened. "I'll tell what ticks me off: when somebody says, 'You're really intelligent. Why are you *just* a waitress?' I got fired once for answering that question with one of my own: 'Why are you *just* an asshole?' I mean, if you're good at what you do, and you like what you're doing, why is it *just*?"

"I agree. If you think of it as 'just', it'll be 'just' for the rest of your life."

"I like people, and I try to make my own art form out of serving them, put a little theater in it. People who think the job makes me a lesser person are less than I am."

"…you really came to Rollo's to hear me play?'

"What you're saying is, it's not the job, it's how you do it that gives it worth. 'It's the Singer not the Song.'"

"Rolling Stones. *December's Children*, 1965."

"What song on it was a hit for both the Stones and Marianne Faithful?"

"'As Tears Go By.'"

"You are good."

I sipped my coffee and looked her up and down. "So, you really came to Rollo's to hear me play."

"I liked you the minute you asked me for a pencil, Sam. I decided a long time ago that when I see something I want, I reach for it. Otherwise, I'd be regretting it for the rest of my days. I know at the end of the week you'll be going back to Pennsylvania, but if I let that happen without reaching for you, I know I'll worse than regret it, win or lose."

She stood and took my empty cup. "It's getting late on your clock. You're going back to Rollo's tonight aren't you?"

"Yeah. If I have to ride in an ambulance."

"I knew you wouldn't let those punks scare you away. Are you sure you're okay?"

"I'm a little sore, but I'm not fuzzy-headed anymore. Never been tased before; it really rattled my brain."

"I saw those guys at Rollo's earlier. What was that all about?"

I told her about bucking the ASWI shakedowns and that I'd caused Whitey some embarrassment at the Crescent, and how that turned it into a vendetta. "I doubt they'll try that again because I'll be watching for them. My guess is they're back in Tennessee by now."

"Maybe, maybe not. Just be careful." She handed me a small jar of makeup and a brush.

"What's this?"

"Something to hide that mouse under your eye. It may look worse later."

Carlotta walked me to the door. She pulled my face down to hers and kissed me long and soft. "So, Sam, do I get a rain check?"

I hesitated, and she picked up on it. "Don't answer that. Let it be a surprise."

XXVI

Back at the room I checked the phone book for a sporting goods store. I owed Rollo's a baseball bat, since the cops confiscated the one I borrowed. Jenny still hadn't called, and when I tried to call her, the call went straight to voice mail. Her phone was off because they were shooting. At least that's what I wanted to think. When I checked my e-mail, I found a message from Ed: four more scenes in the drop box.

I opened the first file. It was an edit of the sensuous waterfall scene, and when it jump cut to me watching from above, I realized why Simon had me take off my hat. The camera caught the thinning hair at the back of my head and my scalp shining through. Simon saw it on the monitor. It was his way of putting me in my place for my attitude.

I decided the other clips could wait.

What I did instead was pull up the pictures Marcie sent. I clicked on one of the office shots she took of Jenny with me studying a page of script changes. Over our shoulders the clock on the wall showed five-thirty. I wished I could reach into that picture and turn the clock back, all the way to the day I took the job.

I tried to call Jenny one more time before I left for Rollo's. It went to voicemail after five rings. That meant the phone was on; she just wasn't answering. "Hi, this is Jenny. Leave a message." The phone beeped and I stared at it for a good ten seconds before I clicked off. I couldn't think of anything I wanted to say.

When I got to Rollo's, I walked in with the new ball bat in my carry bag. I found my guitar intact on the shelf where I left it. Apparently nobody had touched it while I was gone. I always wipe my guitar down with a piece of flannel when I put it away. If anybody else fools with it, their prints show. Not exactly Sherlock Holmes, but when it happens, I know it. I was relieved that I could trust the gang at Rollo's to keep their hands off.

I took the bat out to the bar. Dino, one of the bartenders saw me putting it back in its niche and laughed. "I wondered who borrowed the Adjudicator." He was a lean, blonde-haired beach-bum type, with the likeable cocky attitude Tom Cruise captured in *Cocktail*.

"Brought you a new one."

"What happened to the old one?"

"Don't ask, don't tell."

He laughed and ran his index finger along the side of his nose in the universal gesture of conspiracy. "Understood. How about a beer?"

"Sure. I've got time." I sat at the bar and he ran a draft for me. I was halfway through it when somebody said, "Excuse me. Sam Dunne?"

I turned, wary, and found myself facing the kid I'd heard playing outdoors a few days before. "Yep. You got me."

"My name's Eric Goldsboro." He hesitated but finally held out his hand for me to shake. "I play at Monte's down the beach."

"Good to meet you. I saw you a couple of days ago doing Happy Hour."

"It's my night off. I heard you were playing here, so I thought I'd come down and check it out."

"This scene is a little bit different from your act. I don't do looping or sampling; I just play and sing. People here are big on requests. How do you handle that?"

"I get requests, but I can't always play them. I try to play something by the same artist or in the same style. Or if I'm lucky, the guy gets called to his table before I have to deal with it."

"I used to use MIDI files as backup, but when the crowd gets used to hearing a full sound, playing a song that's not on the stick makes the guitar by itself sound a little thin. So I try to make the guitar as full as I can and run with it. You ever hear Ricky play here?"

"Yeah. He's pretty good, but his show is about ninety percent personality. He's got a line of bullshit a mile long."

"That's Ricky, but that's his strength. Everybody runs a different game. But don't sell him short. He knows one hell of a lot of songs. I've never heard him play the same one twice in one night." Poke. "And it's all from memory." Eric didn't take the bait. But when the crowd turns over every half hour, I guess you can get away with a short repertoire. "I'd better get to it. If you're around when I take a break, come on over. I'll buy you a beer."

The night went pretty well. I was a little distracted at first, watching the crowd for Whitey and his buddies, but I managed to put it aside. If they showed, they showed, and nothing I could do would prevent it. The best thing I could do is let them see that I wasn't going to let them intimidate me. Then I caught myself watching the crowd for Carlotta.

At break time, Eric came over and sat with me. "That's a lot of sound you get from the guitar. Where do you find your arrangements?"

"They're all mine."

"Really?"

"Yeah," I nodded. "You play for forty years, you pick up a few tricks. A lot of my versions came from playing by the seat of my pants when somebody requested a song that was familiar but I never played before. You figure out how you can make it work on the spot. If it looks promising, you woodshed a while later and put it the best form you can. The trick is to work in the little fills and accents you hear on the original recording. Not all the crowd notices, but enough do."

"That's a lot of work."

"Yeah, but when it's your living, the job becomes your life."

The second half of the night went as well as the first. The crowd was noisy and receptive. Around eleven, Eric caught my eye on his way out and waved; still no Carlotta. Then around a quarter to twelve, I saw her come in and take a seat at the bar. She was wearing a tight pair of jeans and a white blouse that contrasted her suntan. She ordered a beer and then sat at a forty-five degree angle to face the stage.

I looked out to her and smiled. She eyed me over the rim of her glass. I started the intro to my song "Lady Will You Stay." It just seemed right.

Lady will you stay, till I put my guitar away

Or will you fade like the final chords of my last melody?

Will you cut and run, or tarry till the sun

Bathes us in its golden morning ray?

When I hit the words of the last verse, Carlotta's glass was down, and the look in her eyes would melt titanium.

My guitar is in its case. Won't you take its place?

Together we could make a symphony.

I ended the song, and sang a chorus of Roy Rogers' "Happy Trails" to hoots and whistles, said goodnight, then climbed off the stage. In the storeroom, I checked my phone. No calls. I shut the damned thing off and headed for the bar.

Five o'clock comes way too fast when you're busy till three.

XXVII

Carlotta left for work and I left her place soon after. I waited till I got back to the Breakers to check my phone. The only call was from a 949 area code, California. The call came at two a.m. I punched in the code for my voice-mail and listened to the message.

"Sam, it's Marcie Graham. I didn't know who else to call. I need to talk to you. It's important. Please call me. It doesn't matter what time it is; I'll keep my cell on."

I thought it over. I have the same suspicion about "call me it's important" as I do about e-mails with "important" or "urgent" in the subject line, but Marcie was a tough kid and the anxiety in her voice convinced me she was in trouble.

She answered on the second ring. "Hold on," she whispered. There was a minute's silence, and then she said in a hushed voice, "I had to get out of the room. I think everybody's still asleep in there, but I can't take the chance."

"Marcie, what's going on?"

"I don't know, Sam, but I'm scared. Something's happened, and I'm not sure what it means."

"What's is it?"

"That cop, Kearny?"

"Yeah, what about him?"

"He got a group of the shots I took around the time Ray was murdered, to see who was where."

I didn't tell her I already knew. "And?"

"I think somebody tampered with the card in the camera."

"They're evidence now. Have you told Kearny?"

"I'm afraid to talk to him. He still thinks I may have murdered Ray."

"And because you took all the pictures, you aren't in any of them to establish your whereabouts."

"Right, and that's not all. There are some pictures on it I never took, and they've been switched with two of the others." She gasped. "Gotta go."

She clicked off and left me staring at the phone. I turned on my computer and while I waited for it to cycle through the start-up, I tried to make sense out of what Marcie said. Somebody was tampering with evidence and the odds were good it was the same person who killed Ray.

I opened my e-mail and found Marcie's message. Then I opened the files one by one and spread them across my screen. What pictures did he switch, and why? And who said it was a he? There were enough weirdoes of both sexes on that crew to go around.

And then I thought about Jenny. She was up there in the middle of them, and in a roundabout way it was my fault. I felt a pang of guilt because of Carlotta. If something happened to her while I was down here, it would be a tough thing to face.

I weighed my options. Do I call Kearny? It would almost be worth it to wake him up at six in the morning. Do I call Jenny? She was ignoring me and maybe wouldn't answer anyway. I decided to wait to see whether Marcie called me back before I did anything else. If she didn't, I'd try calling her.

My stomach was growling. I opted to go to Donovan's for breakfast while I waited. If Marcie called, I could always step outside to talk to her. Carlotta greeted me with a bigger smile than usual and that half-mast eyelid trick women do that starts my meter running.

I dropped into a booth and she poured my coffee. "Hey, sailor. What can I bring you?"

"The usual." I grinned one point shy of a leer.

"You got it." She sashayed away with just a little extra wiggle in her walk. I wasn't the only customer who noticed. I caught at least three other guys appreciating the view. She came by in a minute with the puzzle page of the newspaper. "I'll bet you didn't bring a pencil again."

"Guilty as charged. At least I'm consistent." She dropped a pencil on top of the newspaper and went to the next booth with the coffee pot. I couldn't focus on the Cryptoquote. My mind kept bouncing between Marcie's phone call and Jenny. I was rolling the pencil between my fingers when Carlotta brought my breakfast. "Here's a hint: W equals N."

"You solved it already?"

"Every morning."

"Don't tell me anymore details. I'll develop an inferiority complex."

"Not likely."

My phone buzzed. It was Marcie. "I'd better take this."

She nodded and walked away, but she wasn't smiling. "Marcie?"

There was silence at the other end for about five seconds then a beep as the call ended. I tried calling back, but the call went straight to voice-mail. "Marcie, call me back." Something told me it wasn't smart to say who I was in case somebody else was on her phone. The whole business had me thinking like some secret agent from a bad novel.

"That was short and sweet." Carlotta stood beside me. She smiled. "It's okay, Sam. I know that at any given moment, everybody's attached to somebody, or if not, he's aimed in her direction."

"That call wasn't what you think. It's somebody who may be in trouble, danger even."

"Calling you from California?" She was sharp. But her tone was concern, not antagonism.

"Cell phone. She's in Pennsylvania on the movie set."

"How can you help all the way down here?"

"That's just it. I don't know whether I can. I got a call early this morning and she hung up in the middle. Just now I got a call from her phone, but nobody said anything. Whoever it was hung up after I answered."

She shrugged. "Maybe it's nothing."

I wanted to think so, but in the back of my head, I knew better. When I finished my breakfast, Carlotta brought me the check. "Do I get a big tip today?"

"Sorry, I don't have any fifties, or you'd get them all."

She laughed. "Makes me sound like a hooker."

"No, just greatly appreciated."

XXVIII

Back in my room, I decided to watch the clips Ed sent me. In my opinion, some of them didn't really need music, and I wondered why they sent them at all. A few would have put music in competition with the dialog. Then I thought about the smirk Simon gave me at the fire pit. He was letting me know he had Jenny under his control. The kicker was the tent scene with Bobby and Jenny instead of Janine, played out in the same detail, with my footage intercut as if that's how it had been all along.

It was probably better that I was far away. I'm not sure what would have happened if Simon walked into my room at that moment. He was turning — had turned Jenny into his new Janine in every twisted way. The longer we went without speaking, the more I felt as if I were watching her float away.

If I called Kearny, I had to play it right. If I told him somebody rigged the pictures, he'd run right in and shut everything down. Maybe he'd find the killer, and maybe not. I punched in his number. He answered on the third ring.

"Sam Dunne."

"Did I wake you?"

"Nope."

"That's too bad. I was wondering, since I have a whole day with nothing to do, if you'd e-mail me the pictures you told me about, of the cast and crew at the time of Ray McCarthy's murder."

"And if I ask you why the hell you want them, what would you say?"

"I know them all, by sight if not by name. I might be able to spot something." Silence. "Do you want my help or don't you?"

"You were supposed to help me, then you left town."

"What harm can it do to let me see them?"

"Excuse me if I'm skeptical of your good intentions. I haven't forgotten how you sandbagged me on the Danny Barton case."

He had a point. "What have you got to lose?"

"Nothing, I suppose. Okay, you win. What's the address?"

I gave him the code for my drop box and hoped he didn't use it to download the clips from *Lake Deadly*. It would be bad enough when the film was released. I didn't need Kearny giving his buddies at the station a private screening of Jenny-as-Janine.

"You know, Sam, I've been pretty easy on you so far, and Jenny. Janine DiBasil dies, and suddenly Jenny's the star. I've let that angle lie. Don't stiff me on this."

My jaw set. "Wouldn't dream of it."

He laughed and hung up.

XXIX

Kearny took his time about sending the pictures. It was after lunch when they finally arrived in my drop box. I downloaded the whole group, grateful for the free Wi-Fi, and put them all in a folder on my hard drive. There were twenty-five or thirty of them, and I clicked on the Options button in the file folder: large Icons.

There they were, everybody sitting around the fire like a Boy Scout Camporee. The pictures were numbered serially with DSC prefixes. I scrolled down and saw at the end of the group four pictures taken in the office. Two showed Simon and Elizabeth working at the desk with the wall clock showing nine fifteen. The other two were of Ed and Anya sitting at the desk in the same poses and positions. The clock showed nine-forty. Alibis all around, except for Marcie, who had the misfortune to take all the shots and show up in none of them.

I studied the first shot of Simon and Elizabeth, zooming in and panning all around, looking for a reflection, anything that would prove that she was there when the picture was taken. No luck. A curtainless window reflected the other end of the office like polished onyx, right down to the red LED of a digital clock on one of the filing cabinets, but no Marcie. The second shot of the Odd Couple reflected a slightly different angle that was even further away from the photographer.

Then I pulled up the first picture of Anya and Ed. The angle was roughly the same, and so was the reflection in the dark glass. I pulled up the fourth; same story. The pictures were overlapping, and I spread them out then added the picture of Jenny and me for comparison.

I went back to the file menu. The four office shots had the right numbers, DSC 13047 through DSC 13050, and when I clicked on the properties menu for each and looked at their metadata, the times jibed with the wall clock and identified Marcie's Pentax as the source.

I felt as if I were missing some detail, so I arrayed the office shots on the screen. I stared at them each in its turn, then I looked quickly from one to another. On the third try I noticed one small detail: In the reflection of the digital clock in Simon and Elizabeth's pictures, there were three digits. In Anya and Ed's pictures, there were four.

The numbers were reversed on the clock, but when I zoomed in, I could tell the time: nine-fifteen for Simon and Elizabeth, eleven-twenty-seven for Anya and Ed. Someone had gone to a lot of trouble, rigging the internal clock on the camera and probably a computer as well to reverse engineer pictures that fit in the sequence on the camera card, somebody with a lot of technical know-how. My money was on Anya and Ed.

The evidence was stacking up; Ray's call to Anya's cell phone, now the rigged pictures, and one more thing. When Dick killed Janine, I stopped her from taking the knife from him. If she switched the knife, she could explain her prints on it.

That started me thinking about motive. I'm no psychologist, but I understand revenge. According to Ed, Anya worshipped Simon and to him, she was just a tool, a means to an end. He used her to make his movies and kept all the accolades for himself.

Simon married Elizabeth, the financial engine of the operation. Anya was crushed, and that would have made Elizabeth the obvious target. Maybe that was the key word: obvious. Anya would be first in line as a suspect if Elizabeth were murdered. How to punish Simon? Murder his movie, and in the bargain, kill the focus of Simon's obsession, Tippi Hedren to his Hitchcock, and throw suspicion on the jealous wife.

If Anya were that jealous of Elizabeth, she had to be at least as jealous of Janine, and how better to have her revenge than on camera. Simon had killed Janine in front of the lens a half dozen times, but this time it was for real, and he would have to watch it over and over again. He couldn't help himself.

But how did Ray McCarthy fit into the picture? Did Anya enlist his help in killing Janine? Or did he see something he shouldn't have? Ray was a rat, and I wouldn't put blackmail past him if he saw Anya switch the knives.

And then there was Ed. He worshipped Anya like she worshipped Simon; what part did he have in it all? I thought back to the night of Janine's murder, and yes, that's what it was, murder. Ed was as shocked as anybody when it happened; I was convinced he didn't see it coming. But somebody sat in Ray's passenger seat when his throat was cut. Was it Ed, distracting him while Anya slugged him, or was it Anya who sat beside Ray while Ed cut his throat?

I was sure Marcie didn't take the picture of Anya and Ed. They probably used the auto timer to get in position and have the camera take their alibi pics. Then they put them on the card in place of two others. But Marcie knew, and maybe now Anya and Ed knew that she knew, and if so, she was in danger.

And for that matter, so was Jenny. If Anya's goal was to hurt Simon by killing his picture and killing Janine, would she try again now that the film was revived and Simon had a new Janine?

I could tell Kearny all this, and it would raise questions, but it wasn't enough. I could make a case to him that Anya had motive and opportunity to kill Janine, but I couldn't prove she did it. And the office photos? They didn't really make a case either. If I were under Kearny's microscope, I'd want to fix an alibi too, and the two of them had the know-how to make it look good. After all, it was their job to make the false look real.

My phone rang. It was Marcie's number. I answered it but again didn't say anything. There was silence for a few seconds then, "Sam?" It was Marcie's voice.

"Marcie, are you all right?"

"Yeah, I'm okay. I had to hang up before because I heard someone coming."

"The first time, or the second?"

"What? I only called once."

"Somebody called my number from your phone about ten minutes after I talked to you. If it wasn't you, somebody knows you called me. I want you to do two things, Marcie. First, get out of there. Do you have your own car?"

"No, I rode up with Ed and Anya in the truck. My car's back in Hanniston. But I can't leave. They need me here. They're shooting the lake scenes tonight."

I felt a chill run over me. I saw Janine die, and then I saw the same scene with Jenny's face. I had an idea.

"Can you do something to ding the camera, or screw up any other equipment to stall them tonight?"

"I — I don't know. Why?"

"Trust me, Marcie. You have to do it. Stop them from shooting tonight. Lives are at stake."

"I don't understand."

"I'll explain everything later. And whatever you do, don't go anywhere alone. Keep other people around you. I have to go." I hung up and called the local airport.

A flight was leaving in two hours that would get me to Morgantown, West Virginia by seven after a layover in Lexington, and I could rent a car and drive To Lost Creek in another hour. The sun wouldn't set till at least eight o'clock, so they wouldn't be filming any sooner than nine. With luck I could make it there before they started shooting, even if Marcie couldn't delay them. I made my flight reservation and went online to book a rental car. The best Budget could give me was a Chevy Sonic. I hoped I could fit in it.

Maybe I was crazy to think I could make a difference, but I had to do it. I'd need some help, and the only person I had was Carlotta. I rang the bell at her apartment praying she was home. She opened the door and the smile that spread across her face was like a sunrise. It faded when I told her what I had to do.

I told her the story of the sound track job, of the murders, of Jenny's involvement, and the evidence that pointed to Anya as the killer. "There's not enough to prove anything, but I know in my gut Jenny's in danger, and Marcie too. I have to go back there."

"Can't you call the cops, this Kearny guy?"

"I will, but the film crew has moved out of his jurisdiction. He can try to call in the West Virginia State Police or the locals in Lost Creek, but without hard evidence, his hands are tied."

"What can you do?"

"I don't even know, but I feel like I have to do something."

"How can I help?"

"I have a flight to catch in less than two hours. Can you take me to the airport?"

"Sure. I'll be glad to."

"I have to make one more stop. I have to tell Jake, the manager at Rollo's, what's going on."

I found Jake in his office. I was beginning to think that he slept under his desk.

"Jake, I have some bad news."

He looked up, glaring, from a pile of receipts.

"I have to go back to Pennsylvania. It's an emergency."

"No, you don't." He shoved back his chair and stood up, fists clenched. "We have a contract."

"Did you read it?" His forehead creased in a puzzled frown. "Maybe you saw the clause about emergencies." Ricky had included a clause in his standard contract that was essentially an escape hatch if something dire came up; an accident, a death in the family, or an impending one. Some club owners may have seen it and insisted on striking it, but apparently Jake hadn't.

I pushed a copy of the contract with the emergency clause circled in red across the desk. "Read it for yourself. I'm out of here."

"What's this big emergency? You come down with the 'green flu'?" Management's euphemism for calling in sick to take a higher paying gig.

"No. It's literally a matter of life and death."

"You son of a bitch. You can't just leave me hanging."

"I'm not." I set another piece of paper on the desk. "I called the AF of M local. There's a list of five people who can work in my place. Take your pick. I'll pick up the tab."

"You still owe me one more night."

"And you'll get it. Just not tonight. I'll be back."

Jake started around his desk, his lip curled in a snarl.

"Before you make a big mistake, one question. Did you read the article in *Nightside*? If you did, you know my back story. Don't push this." I hated to play that card, but it worked. His fists unclenched, and he tried to stare me down, but it didn't work.

"Get out of here."

"That was my intention. I'm glad we finally agree."

Joey would scream, but Ricky would understand.

Carlotta drove me to the airport and waited with me until it was time to go through security and board the flight. As I headed for the scanners, she grabbed my hand. "Come back to me, Sam. Come back safe." I bent and kissed her. "Rain check."

XXX

ost times, I find cell phones a curse, but this time, mine came in handy. Marcie had texted the name and address of the farm where Last Light was filming, and I was able to get a pretty good fix on its location and driving directions from Mapquest.

I had no baggage, which earned me the fish eye and a pat down from a TSA worker. My looks probably didn't help my case, either. He seemed almost disappointed that I wasn't carrying a brick of C-4 in my hip pocket. He must have been low on his monthly quota.

The flight was torture. Sun Crest Airlines flies refurbished DC-10s with reconfigured seating that kept me folded in a tight, cramping Z. And halfway to Lexington, we flew through a thunderstorm that shook the plane like a washing machine full of throw rugs. Besides that, Sun Crest had a strict no-cell-phone policy that kept me incommunicado till we touched down in Kentucky.

I sat at a Starbucks in the concourse of Blue Grass Airport and pulled out my phone. As I expected, no one called. I tried Jenny's number and my call went straight to voice mail. Her phone was off, which meant they were probably on the set. I took a chance that she might turn it on to check her messages. "Jen, it's Sam. You're in danger." Who did I name as the source? Ed? Anya? Elizabeth? I kept it short and simple. "Don't do the shoot tonight. Play sick, throw a tantrum, any excuse. Just don't do it. I'll explain later." As I clicked off, I worried that she wouldn't hear the message, and I worried even more that she'd hear it and ignore it.

I hesitated to call Kearny but did anyway. Voice mail again. "Mike, this is Sam Dunne. I need to talk to you right away. Call me."

I tried Marcie's number. No answer again. Strike three. But of course, if they were shooting, her phone would be off the same as Jenny's. I didn't leave a message in case whoever played with her phone earlier did it again.

The wait for my connecting flight was one of the most frustrating times I've spent in my life. I couldn't do anything but sit and wait while the wheels turned without me. And when I got there, then what? I didn't know for sure who to watch or what to watch for. And I couldn't carry so much as a nail clipper on the airplane.

I wouldn't have time to hunt down a gun shop in Morgantown, and even if I found one, they couldn't sell me a squirt gun without the mandatory

No answer...strike three...

waiting period. I looked across the concourse and saw a magazine counter that doubled as a convenience store full of souvenir junk and small items travelers might find handy.

Near the register I found what I wanted. Bic pens. I bought two; one for each hand. As I paid for them, I realized that the pens would look as suspicious to the TSA Brownshirts as any potential weapon if I had no reason to be carrying them. I bought a notebook.

Before I got on the plane to Morgantown, I checked my phone one last time. No calls. Where the hell was Kearny?

XXXI

The weather had cleared, and the last leg of the flight was a lot calmer than the first. The Chevy Sonic wasn't as bad as I thought it would be once I pushed the seat back as far as it would go. I switched on my phone to pull up my driving directions and got a No Service message. It called to mind all those cell service ads that showed a big white West Virginia-shaped blank in the coverage area.

I snagged a road map from the rental agency and headed for I-79. I'd have to keep checking my phone every few minutes in the hope that I'd pick up a signal along the way. "Almost Heaven, West Virginia," my ass. John Denver never tried to use a cell phone out here.

The sun set about ten times in the next hour, dipping below the peaks and ridges and popping out again as I drove between them. In spite of its faults, West Virginia can boast the best highways in the country, courtesy of the late Senator Robert C. Byrd, whose name is on just about every park, public building, and drinking fountain in the state.

I drove through Lost Creek as twilight set in. I got directions twice from locals, neither time exactly accurate, but I managed to find Martin Farms on a two-lane blacktop road fifteen miles from the Interstate. I was looking for a place to turn around. I thought I must have made a wrong turn but around the next bend, I saw the sign: Martin Farms Pure - Bred Holsteins. Someone had hand painted Last Light on drooping cardboard and nailed it to a fencepost at the stile.

Ed chose the location well. Not only did it take the whole crew out of Kearny's official reach, the place was so remote it was almost inaccessible.

The gate wasn't padlocked, but I still had to get out of the Sonic to open it and close it behind me. As an afterthought, I slipped the shackle through the hasp and snapped the lock shut. Nobody was going to make a fast getaway down this road.

The close growth of pines on either side of the road made a black trench with the fading violet sky overhead. A half mile in, the trees gave onto a meadow and beyond it; I saw the silhouettes of a barn, two silos and a big gabled house with lights in the windows. A dozen or so cars were parked in the yard in front of the barn, and I recognized Ed's Tahoe as my headlights flashed over it.

As I unfolded myself out of the Sonic, a rent-a-cop in a khaki uniform strolled over, shining a flashlight in my face.

"Can I help you?" That's the security guard's diplomatic way of saying, "Who the hell are you and what the hell are you doing here?"

"I'm Sam Dunne. I'm writing the soundtrack for *Lake Deadly*. Where are they shooting?"

He took a step back and keyed the mic on his epaulet. "Pulaski here. Got a guy named Sam Dunne just pulled in. Is he on the list?"

After a moment's pause, the speaker crackled and a harsh voice said, "He's cleared."

Pulaski lowered his flashlight. It was one of those six-cell jobs that double as a nightstick. "Do you have some I.D.?"

I showed him my driver's license and he was satisfied. "They're filming about a quarter mile from here. Follow the road on the other side of the barn to the lake. You'll have to walk." He wasn't kidding. The ruts were deep enough that I would have torn the oil pan off the Sonic, if I didn't hang it up first.

I heard the generator humming before I saw the lights from the shoot. The crew kept it at a distance so that the noise wouldn't interfere with the filming. I followed the power cable and in a minute or two I saw the glow of the halogen work lights through the trees. They weren't filming at the moment, so the big ones were off.

Jenny and Robby were standing waist deep in a lake just a little bit smaller than the one at Tuscarora. Both were nude, and to Jenny's credit, she at least kept her arms crossed over her chest. She couldn't see me behind the work lights, and that was just as well.

Ed was circulating with his clipboard. Simon was behind the camera, adjusting its angle while Smith stood by. I couldn't see Anya, but I figured she had to be there somewhere. Marty was holding the mannequin Lake Thing, knife hilt sticking from its chest, beside them. They had apparently already filmed the stabbing scene and were preparing to shoot the climax. I felt a tug at my sleeve. It was Marcie.

"Sam. I didn't expect you to be here."

"Neither did anyone else. Get me up to speed."

"After I talked to you, I dinged one of the connectors to the sound cable, but I guess when Ed bought a replacement for the old one, he bought a spare. I couldn't slow things down at all. But I did manage to get this."

She handed me a data card and said quietly. "It's from the Pentax. It's been reformatted. All the production stills are gone."

"Are you sure it's the same card?"

She nodded. "It's marked with an inventory number like all the digital media. I remember the number, three-five-seven to identify the project, the camera and the content. Fetus and I joked about playing it on the Daily Number but never got around to it, and it hit two days later."

Somebody tripped over an extension cord toppling one of the work lights. It fell inches short of the water. Grips scurried to right it again as Ed shouted, "Goddamn it, watch your feet."

"I see Ed. Where's Anya?"

"She's gone. Simon and Anya had a big blowup this morning and she quit."

"Quit? Over what?"

"Simon wasn't happy about how she was running things. He said she was filming Jenny from unflattering angles. He all but accused her of trying to make Jenny look bad. He's doing the PD job himself."

So Simon took over. He wanted Jenny filmed exactly according to his vision, and Anya wasn't cooperating. If Anya was gone, who else should I watch? At that moment, Dick Hunter walked into the light as the female version of the Lake Thing, one shriveled dug hanging from the rags that swaddled its chest.

"Okay folks. Places." Ed was calling the shot. Robbie crouched to go under the water. Jenny's face contorted into a look of sheer pain. She was a better actress than I thought she would be. Seeing her in an identical tableau as Janine's made me shudder.

"Strike." The lights came on.

"Rolling." Robby leaned forward into the water and the female Lake Thing moved behind Jenny and reached around with the knife.

"Hold it, Hunter," Simon said. "Keep rolling. The angle's not right. Alton," At least the pervert didn't call her Jenny. "Bend your knees under the water. Lower yourself. You're a little taller than Janine was."

I flashed on Janine standing beside Jenny. "No she isn't," I said, and set off at a run, splashing into the lake, an uncapped Bic pen in either hand.

"Hey, what the hell—get out of the shot!" Ed shouted.

The monster turned its head and gave me enough time to come up behind it and drive the points of both pens into its shoulders. There were two screams, one when the pens stabbed deep into the creature's flesh and the other when its knife hand jerked and slashed Jenny across her collarbone.

I wrestled the knife from the Lake Thing's hand and tore off its face, revealing Anya's underneath. Everyone stood stunned as I dragged Anya toward the shore. I held her hand palm out and said, "Let's try that trick again." I drew the knife across Anya's palm and a weal of blood formed from the wound.

Simon stepped around the camera. "Savage, what the hell are you doing?"

"You bastard," she hissed. "I worshipped you, slaved for you and made your movies what they are, and what thanks do I get? You marry that bean counter. And it was bad enough you fawned over that slut DiBasil, but after I got rid of her, you found another doll to play with."

Simon stammered, "I—I—"

The gunshot made everyone jump. Ed had fired the first one in the air, but by the time I looked in his direction, he was aiming his revolver at me. "Let her go, Sam. Now."

"You killed Ray McCarthy. He saw Anya switch the knives."

"What does it matter now? I'm taking Anya and we're leaving, and I'll kill anybody who tries to stop me."

"No you won't. Drop the gun." Kearny stepped from the shadows, his Glock leveled at Ed. Ed wheeled in panic and fired at Kearny. His shot went wild. Kearny's didn't. Ed fell to his knees then face forward onto the shore. Kearny kicked the revolver away and rolled him over. Ed's breath came in wet, sucking gasps through the hole in his chest.

Kearny shouted, "Does anybody have a phone that works out here? Call 911."

I dragged Anya to the shore. She was shuddering, moaning. She sat heavily on the shore arms around her knees and started to rock back and forth and wail. The rest of the crew stood like statues, people who made pretend violence and gore for a living, stunned by the real thing.

"Where the hell did you come from?" I asked Kearny, who had ripped open Ed's shirt and was using a wad of the cloth to stanch the wound in his chest.

"Just got here. After you asked to see the pictures, I gave them another look."

"You saw the clock?"

"Yeah. It wasn't enough to make a case on its own. I was going to come by myself on my own dime, since this is out of my bailiwick, maybe shake a confession out of these two, but DeVon insisted on tagging along."

"Where is he now?"

Kearny jerked his head over his shoulder. "He's back there. We took a path through the woods instead of the road and I tripped over Hunter. He was knocked out and stripped to his bathing suit."

"Anya."

"Things wouldn't have gotten this far, but some jackass locked the gate at the main road and we had to walk in."

I didn't say a word.

"I thought you were in Myrtle Beach."

"Took a day off. I just couldn't stay away."

"When were you going to tell me about the clock?"

"Check your voice-mail. I tried to call you before I got into the Dead Zone."

"Uh-huh." Kearny's tone and his look told me I'd be hearing about it later, and I'd be hearing a lot.

I stood and turned to see Marcie wiping the blood from Jenny's chest. Our eyes met, and Jenny looked away. I picked up a terrycloth robe I recognized as hers and took it over. I was going to wrap it around her shoulders, but she held out her hands to take it from me, pre-empting my gesture. Her eyes were glassy. I told Marcie, "She's going into shock. Sit her down before she falls."

Devon stepped into the light, his thick fingers wrapped around a stumbling Hunter's arm. "Looks like I missed the party."

Simon turned to Smith, and I heard him say, "Still rolling?"

XXXII

I found Razor in the upper deck of Carson Stadium indulging his second passion to playing the guitar, watching the Hanniston Wildcats, our local minor league baseball team. He was sitting in the cheap seats with a cardboard tray of nachos and a beer.

Razor is arguably the best metal guitarist in the Hanniston area, playing lead for the local group Blood Lightning, a steelyard band that fuses sixties rhythm and blues with hardcore thrash. He's also Hanniston's most accomplished thief. He could unlock my van, start it, and drive it away without a key as easily and quickly as I could with one. With Razor, there was no breaking, just entering.

Today, he was sitting in the sun in the middle of a block of empty seats, his Chuck Taylor Converses propped on the row in front of him. His shoulder length dirty blond hair was pulled up under a red Wildcats ball cap, and mirrored shades hid his eyes. I came down the ramp from behind him, but he waved to acknowledge me before I even entered his peripheral vision.

"Sam Dunne."

"Razor. How's the metal business?"

"Rusting away. The wheel's turning again. Crowds are yelling for Jurassic Rock these days; Credence Clearwater Revival, John Cougar, ZZ Top. We can play it, but it has no soul. You?"

"Still pickin' and grinnin'."

The crowd cheered as one of the Wildcats hit the ball over the right field fence. Neither of us spoke for a minute or two; then I said, "I need some help."

He nodded, eyes never leaving the field. "Okay, fill me in."

"I need somebody found, and once I find him, I need a few things to make him wish I hadn't."

"Why not just have it done? I know a few people who work cheap."

I shook my head. "It has to be me, and he has to know it's me while it happens."

"Oh, honor and *hubris*, huh?"

"Something like that."

"What's it all about?"

For the next half hour I told Razor about Whitey, ASWI, Mike and Toni's, The Crescent Inn, and the encounter at Myrtle Beach. When I finished, he said, "I never ran into ASWI. I guess they never come into Bendik's."

"Maybe they want to stay alive." I laughed at the thought of Whitey and his beehived partner trying to shake down the meanest biker bar in Pennsylvania.

"They sound like typical jackals; cull the weakest out of the herd and have them for dinner." He tipped back his cup and chugged the last of his beer. "You have the same cell number?"

"Yeah."

"Give me a day or so. I'll get back to you."

I left the stadium and as I started the car, I realized that during the whole exchange, Razor never looked in my direction, but he'd find Whitey if anyone could.

When Razor called, I didn't recognize the number. He changes his cell phone every three or four weeks. "Found your boy. He and some broad are skulking around the bars in Keyser, Maryland this week. They're staying in separate rooms in the Pine Lodge Motel. She's in 214 and he's in 203."

"How'd you find all that so fast?"

Razor chuckled. "A good magician never reveals his secrets. You owe me two hundred bucks for that one. I have to pay my sources."

"You ought to be a private eye."

He shrugged. "What, and give up music?"

"Did you get the equipment?"

"Tomorrow. If you don't mind, I'm going to tag along with you. Looks like fun. Besides, you're probably out of practice at picking locks. I did my homework. The Pine Lodge has security cams, and you don't want to be caught on video tinkering with somebody's doorknob for five minutes."

XXXIII

It was around two-thirty when I heard the sound of a loud muffler outside. Razor and I had been waiting in the dark for about three hours in room 203 of the Pine Lodge Motel in Keyser, Maryland. I pulled the drapes back an inch and saw Whitey get out one side of his van and some skinny little blonde with horn rimmed glasses climb out of the other.

They walked together up the steps to the second level and she turned right at the landing while Whitey turned left toward 203. Whitey's key clicked in the lock, and the door swung inward. I stood behind it.

Whitey threw his keys on the table and kicked the door shut before he turned on the lights. He blinked when he saw Razor slumped in a chair across the room, one of his long legs dangling over its arm. He grinned and raised a can of Budweiser in a salute. "Evenin'."

"Who the hell are you? What are you doing here?"

"Nothing much," Razor said, standing with a practiced casual insouciance. "I'm just here to unlock the door. The guy you need to worry about is behind you." He pointed to me standing in the corner and Whitey turned. His hand reached behind his back, but before he could get what he wanted, he got something he didn't. I zapped him with the taser and he fell to the floor like he'd been poleaxed.

He twitched a little bit and a silver string of drool ran from the corner of his mouth. I stood over him and let the taser work its pulsing magic. That's the difference between a taser and a stun gun. The stun gun delivers one jolt and has to recharge before you can dish out another. A taser can keep hitting the recipient with pulse after pulse.

I reached under Whitey and pulled the .38 revolver from its holster in his waistband. I tossed the pistol to Razor, who shoved it into the pocket of his windbreaker. I reached into my jacket and pulled out a straight razor. I bent over Whitey and held it in his line of vision. A flick of my thumb, and the blade swiveled out of the mother of pearl handle like a switchblade, a piece of theater I learned from drug lord Tiny Settles. Whitey's eyes got wide. He wasn't so out of it that he didn't recognize mortal peril when he saw it.

I set the taser on the floor and put a knee in Whitey's chest, grabbing his chin with my other hand and turning his head to face me. I held the razor at the corner of his eye. "You made a big mistake in Myrtle Beach, Asswipe. You misjudged me." I gave him a wicked grin. "I'm crazy."

He opened his mouth, but no words came out.

"I could kill you, and you wouldn't be the first. But I have a better idea." I pinned his head against the shabby carpet and dragged the razor over his head from his brow to his crown, pass after pass, dry shaving his scalp. When I was through, the rooster crest of his ducktail lay on the rug in a pile of white fluff like milkweed and his scalp was raw and bleeding.

Razor looked over my shoulder. "Nice. Kind of a reverse Mohawk."

"The Stephen Wright look."

I leaned in an inch from Whitey's nose. "Remember, I caught you alone once, and I can do it again. Stay out of my business. Stay out of my life." I stood up. Razor rifled Whitey's pockets and found his cell phone and the keys to his van. He popped the back off the phone and took out the battery then carried it and the keys into the bathroom. I heard the toilet flush.

Razor came back and with the flick of his thumb, flipped the blade out of his knife. He doubled the cord from the motel phone into a loop and cut it. "Seems the phones are out of order. Don't get foolish ideas about calling the law. They might forward the call to the Myrtle Beach P.D."

When we left, Whitey still lay in the middle of the floor and would probably be there a while.

XXXIV

If you've been keeping up with current events, you know that Ed and Anya were charged with murder one and are waiting for trial. Anya's pleading insanity. Too bad for Ed he couldn't plead stupidity.

Simon got his wish. *Lake Deadly* was rushed to completion and because of its notoriety enjoyed a modest run in the theaters before it went to cable and video. Joe Bob Briggs gave it three-and-a-half stars and said, "Check it out." Last Light sent me a copy, but I still haven't watched it.

Elizabeth and Simon honored my contract in spite of our differences, and I'll be getting residuals into my old age. Speaking of cable, Simon's documentary, *The Lake Deadly Murders* was picked up by HBO. He used some of my leftover music from the movie for the documentary flick too.

I heard Wendy Conn was turned down by the same people when she pitched them a special about the "Sam Dunne Jinx." The producers told her to get back to them if I killed anybody else.

The last time I talked to Mike and Kelli, they hadn't heard from ASWI. I'm betting they never will again.

The slash across Jenny's collarbone healed with almost no scarring, but Simon said it made her an even hotter attraction. He and Elizabeth have taken over managing her career and have her auditioning for lots of roles. You may have also heard that Jenny moved out of the apartment two days after Anya tried to kill her. She went to L.A. with the Last Light entourage chasing fame, fortune, and stardom. I wasn't invited along. The last time I talked to Jenny, she told me she was headed for Las Vegas to do another film for Simon, a Tom Willis script called *Gore Casino*, and she didn't know when she'd be back in Hanniston.

The last time I talked Carlotta, she rolled over, kissed me, and said goodnight.

THE END

ABOUT OUR CREATORS

AUTHOR –

FRED ADAMS, JR. is a retired Penn State University English Professor who spends his days writing pulp fiction and his nights working as a singer songwriter. His Sam Dunne novel *Dead Man's Melody* was nominated as Pulp Novel of the Year in 2017's Pulp Factory Awards, his Smith Brothers novel *The Eye of Quang-Chi* was nominated for the same award in 2018, and *Holster Full of Death*, a Dead Sheriff novel, was a 2019 nominee. His titles include *Hitwolf* 1 and 2; *Six Gun Terrors* vols. 1, 2, and 3; *C.O. Jones: Mobsters and Monsters, Skinners*, and *The Damned and the Doomed*, and *Bloody Key*, an Ike Mars novel. A sampler anthology, *Fred Adams, Jr: Pulp Writer*, new stories featuring his series characters was published by Airship 27 in 2019. His original Sherlock Holmes anthology *The Affair of the Chronic Argonaut* was recently published by Pro Se Press. Forthcoming titles from Airship 27 include *C.O. Jones: Home Front, Six Gun Terrors 4: The Town Killers, Wired*, an Ike Mars novel, and *Featherstone of Lloyd's*. He lives in Mount Pleasant, Pennsylvania "in "perpetual terror of boredom."

Visit Fred's website at http://drphreddee.com/author

INTERIOR ILLUSTRATOR –

RICHARD JUN – is an aspiring comic book illustrator and a professional doctor of optometry. He spent most of his formative years poring over comics books. He carefully and meticulously copied the likes of Art Adams, John Buscema, John Byrne and Jim Lee. He majored in drawing and painting at Loyala University in Chicago and was awarded scholarship to attend summer classes at the Art Institute of Chicago. After graduation, Rich worked odd jobs but struggles to crack the art world. Keen at making his own way in the world independent from his parents, he went to graduate school to become an eye doctor. He ventured off to New York City for graduate school and loved every minute of it. Rich has spent the last ten years treating patients from eye diseases and preventing blindness. All the while, he continued his affair with comic book and action figures.

Rich lives in Madison Wisconsin with his lovely girlfriend and two rescued pit bulls. One day while perusing the mail, they came across a comic book art class. She encouraged him to jump in and everything changed. Rich met his instructor, Jeff Butler, and continued to study with him for two years. Under Jeffr's tutelage, his aspirations have reignited.

COVER ARTIST -

ROB DAVIS - began his professional art career doing illustrations for role-playing games in the late 1980s. Not long after, he began lettering and inking, then penciling comics for a number of small black and white comics publishers- most notably for Eternity Comics, which eventually became Malibu Comics in the 1990s. His first popular/acclaimed work was SCIMIDAR with writer R.A. Jones at Eternity. Branching out to other black and white publishers and eventually working at both DC and Marvel, Rob worked on likeness intensive comics like TV show adaptations of QUANTUM LEAP and STAR TREK's many incarnations primarily on the DEEP SPACE NINE comics for Malibu. At Marvel he worked on the Saturday morning cartoon based comic book series PIRATES OF DARK WATER. After the comics industry implosion in the late 1990s, Rob picked up work on video games, advertising illustrations and T-shirt design as well as some small press comics like ROBYN OF SHERWOOD for Caliber. Rob continues to do the occasional self-published comic book as well as publisher and designer for his small-press production REDBUD STUDIO COMICS. Rob is Art Director, Designer and Illustrator for the New Pulp production outfit AIRSHIP 27 partnered with writer/editor Ron Fortier. Rob is the two-time recipient of the PULP FACTORY AWARD for "Best Interior Illustrations" for his work on the anthology series SHERLOCK HOLMES: CONSULTING DETECTIVE and has been nominated repeatedly for the same award over the years. Retired from "real work" he lives in central Missouri with his wife, Theresa.

BOOKS BY FRED ADAMS JR.

FRED ADAMS JR. PULP WRITER

SIX-GUN TERRORS Volume One
SIX-GUN TERRORS   Volume Two
SIX-GUN TERRORS Volume Three – The Slithering Terror

HITWOLF
HITWOLF 2 – The Pack

C.O. JONES
C.O. JONES – Skinners
C.O. JONES – The Damned and the Doomed

(SAM DUNNE MYSTERIES)
Dead Man's Melody
Blood is the New Black

(THE SMITH BROTHERS SERIES)
The Eye of Quang Chi

(IKE MARS MYSTERIES)
The Bloody Key

Find these and other great pulp-style books at airship27hangar.com